When Sparks Fly

ANNE KEMP

For my sister, Karen.
*Thank you for **always** being there!*
Love you,
Annie xo

Special Acknowledgements

A special thank you goes out to the folks who follow me on social media or are on my newsletter list. These are the people who I adore asking for help with something for my books, like I did for this one!

The estate where Maisey and Jack's romance takes place is loosely based on the Biltmore Estate in North Carolina. I needed a name for this hotel and I was stumped! So I went to TikTok (where all good ideas come from these days) and asked my village for help. Boy, did they deliver!

Thank you
Leah Hassan-D'Amico
&
Nicole Mcclymont

for both suggesting the name Mistletoe Lodge. I LOVE it! Enjoy reading When Sparks Fly.

CHAPTER 1

Maisey

"911, what's your emergency?"

Gripping my phone, I sigh and attempt a slow calming breath while closing my eyes. There's a crackle in the background as my fireplace works its magic on this cold winter's night—and why, yes, there *is* an emergency I need to attend to.

"Hey, Connie," I manage, drawing out her name into two long syllables. "I didn't know you'd be working tonight. How are you?"

"Maisey! Is that you?" the familiar voice sings in my ear. Connie has worked as the emergency services operator here in Lake Lorelei for years. If you call for help in this town, she's literally the one who answers. I love hearing her stories about some of the insane emergencies she's had to field over the years —like the time my friend Ari got her hand stuck in a toilet. Ooof. She's still trying to live that one down, but Connie can't let it go. Made her year to answer that call.

"It's me. I'm in a bit of a bind, though, and I need"—I swallow big and hard before saying this next word—"help."

"Oh, wow." Connie clucks. "Maisey, it's gotta be bad if you're asking for help. Do you need an ambulance?"

Glancing down at my feet, I roll my eyes. This was supposed to be a relaxing night in. Order a pizza, get the fire going, grab my book, chill. My, how things can go off course.

"Mmmmm, maybe, but it's probably more of a fire department thing. I think."

"You think?" Connie laughs. "What have you done?"

"I was running around all day. So, when I came home I got out my foot massager…"

"Oh, the fancy one you splurged for?" Connie all but crows in my ear. She was in the cafe last year when I ordered it, so she knows how big of a deal it was for me to get it. I'm not one to make expensive and unnecessary purchases. "I love that thing."

"Me, too, except not tonight. I had about five minutes of enjoyment before the tiny knobs digging into the undersides of my feet came to a full stop." Glaring at my feet, I shake my head. "Screeched to a halt."

"So." She takes a giant breath in, and I can imagine her cheeks starting to flush bright pink from her giddiness. "You're saying you're trapped in your foot massager and can't get out?"

For love of all things sugar, Connie can be an angel, but right now she's the devil in disguise.

"Pretty much what I'm trying to say." There. I admitted it out loud. "Connie, I'm stuck in my fancy foot massager."

"Oh, this is good." She snorts, and it reminds me of a cat trying to dislodge a furball. I hear her fingers tapping on a keyboard on the other end of the line, in between her chuckles, that is. Chuckles. Yes, I think Connie's going to get a new nickname. "Okay, I've got Truck 41 swinging by to see what they can do. They've been out on a call but will stop by your place on the way back to the station." She pauses before continuing. "As long as this isn't life-threatening?"

I choose to ignore her snickering. "No. Just painful, uncomfortable, and really awkward. And I need to go to the bathroom."

"You're lucky you even had your cell phone nearby, Maisey. Imagine if you had left it across the room." Connie cackles. "How would you have called, then?"

"Thanks, Connie, you always find the bright side, don't ya?" This woman. Now that she knows this, the whole town will also know. My regulars at breakfast tomorrow are going to have a heyday with this one. "Is there an estimated time for when they might come by?"

"Probably in the next twenty minutes. Hang in there."

The ding-dong-ding of my doorbell makes me jump a mile. It seems my crosstown companion hears it as well.

"Oh my—was that your *doorbell*? How are you..." Connie shrieks with laughter, but I get the last laugh 'cause I hang up on her. Which is probably a stupid move because she was my lifeline until the fire department gets here.

My stomach rumbles, reminding me I ordered a pizza which is probably at my front door right now. The doorbell rings again, and this time my phone lights up as well with a text from an unknown number. It's the pizza guy wanting to know why I'm not answering.

I can see the door from where I'm sitting, so I decide to handle this the old-fashioned way. I yell. "I'm in here, I just can't open the door!"

A few beats pass before I hear someone on the other side. "Uh...okay. Should I bring it in?"

Of course, I've already thought of the fact that, if the door was unlocked, yes he could come in and not only bring me my pizza, but potentially help release me from my foot prison.

However, I'm a bit OCD about locking my doors, and I can see from here that all three locks are in place.

"No, um…I can't get there to let you in." How do I explain to this guy, who is probably some sixteen-year-old working part time, that I'm trapped? The answer is easy. I don't. "Do you mind leaving it at the door?"

"I'll put it on the bench for you, ma'am." Adding insult to injury, I was just called ma'am.

"Thanks, I'll make sure to drop a tip off for you this week."

"Okay. Thanks." Another beat passes before I hear the voice again. "Should I call anyone for you, lady? Do you need help?"

I throw my head back on the soft padding of the chair and stare at the ceiling.

"No. No one you can call, but thanks anyway. The fire department should be here soon."

A door opens and closes in my driveaway, and a car engine turns over, a signal that another lifeline is now gone and I am left waiting on the local firefighters to come to my aid.

Which means, more likely than not, that Jack McCoy will probably be walking through my door any second.

My skin prickles with irritation when I think about him, but luckily he doesn't get to invade my thoughts for very long. The vibration of my cell phone going off next to me grabs my attention. Seeing my friend Dylan's name pop up, I'm grateful for the reprieve, so I answer.

"Did I hear Connie say that you're trapped in your foot massager?"

Seriously? Next time I have a special announcement, forget paying for advertising in the local paper or on the radio, I'll tell Connie. "Please tell me you happen to be in her office and she didn't just blast this out on the Lake Lorelei town Facebook page?"

"I stopped into the station to see my dad, but he's out on a call." Dylan giggles. "Don't worry, Connie is busy telling anyone who'll listen that you're at home, both feet trapped, and can't get out."

"As long as it provides her some entertainment, but I gotta ask: isn't there some kind of privacy act that woman is supposed to uphold?"

"Nice try." Dylan chuckles. "You know it won't stop Connie. Do you want me to come by?"

I love that I've become such good friends with Dylan. She moved to Lake Lorelei about a year or so ago to be closer to her dad. She worked in Los Angeles managing high-end events for the rich and famous, but she always wanted to be a paramedic. Growing up with a father who was a fireman in LA before he moved east, I can see where she got her inspiration from.

"That's okay; Connie said the truck was out on a call and they're coming by. Which means your dad will probably be here soon. Should I tell him you're waiting for him?"

"Ha," Dylan laughs. "You can tell him I need to talk to him, but I'm going home now to do some work. Let him know to call me, please? It'll save me the energy it takes to write him a note."

I know Dylan appreciates the small-town vibe of Lake Lorelei as much as I do. We both lived in bigger cities for a long time. I went to college in San Francisco and made it my home for several years, only staying when I got a job working with one of the most renowned pastry chefs in the area.

But when it came time to leave, I left and did it fast, and I have never looked back. At least not on purpose.

"Why are you going home to work now?" A quick look at my watch tells me it's time for more important things. Things that only Dylan and I enjoy, like the latest reality show pitting uber-rich housewives against each other, even though they're "friends." "It's almost time for our show..."

"And it's the reunion tonight." Dylan lets out a breath. "Man, I'll have to watch it online later. I agreed to plan a wedding for a couple who live in Asheville, and they told me about this contest the Mistletoe Lodge is doing. Do you know about it?"

"The Mistletoe?" Hearing her say Mistletoe Lodge, my ears perk up and I sit a little taller in my recliner. "No, but tell me. What is it?"

"You know how they do that Christmas village on steroids every year?"

Do I? I DO. "You bet your life I know. I love that place at Christmas!"

"It is a bit of a winter wonderland, isn't it? They're asking for engaged couples to submit an essay to win a romantic weekend escape on them. The Mistletoe Lodge wants a love story, so the winning essay gets a weekend away for Christmas celebrations at the estate, two nights' accommodation—all on the house."

"Wow." I let out a low, slow whistle of appreciation. "That's a great prize. All you have to do is write an essay and you're entered?"

"That and be engaged. A true love story, like Wallis Simpson and King Edward."

"Or like Prince Harry and Meghan?" Judging by Dylan's tone, she's not in agreement. A true Britophile, Dylan has followed the royal family through the years.

"I have opinions about them, so moving on." She exhales heavily in my ear. "I'll be working with my clients tonight to write up their story to enter."

Glancing over at a photo that sits in a silver picture frame on the fireplace mantel, my gears start grinding. I love the Mistletoe Lodge. It's a love which has been handed down to me from my mother, because it was her favorite place for us to go to every Christmas as kids. Even after we'd grown up, if my sister or I was in town for the holidays, we would go with Mom to the Mistletoe Lodge. It was our holiday tradition up until the year my mother succumbed to Alzheimer's. The year when everything changed exponentially.

"Can anyone enter this contest?" Putting the phone in my lap, I switch it to speakerphone and pull up the Mistletoe Lodge's website.

"As far as I know." Dylan pauses, her voice low when she speaks again. "Why? Are you going to enter?"

"I don't have a fiancé the last time I checked, and I don't have a love story unless I write about my love for the Red Bird. Seeing as the Red Bird is the cafe my mother left me in her will, I doubt the marketing team at the Mistletoe Lodge will see it as a true tale of falling in love."

"You can try it. Or throw caution to the wind and write up a fake story."

Now she's talking. Scanning the frame on the mantel again, my insides bubble with a warmth of nostalgia. I need to go to the Mistletoe Lodge. Need. Scrolling the website, I see the prizes Dylan mentioned, but also the one item I really hoped would be there: a private tour of the Mistletoe's art collection.

"I like having options. Maybe I can write about my love of pizza? Like the one sitting outside my door right now, waiting for me."

"Oh my god." Dylan sounds like she's choking. "See, I should have come over. I could have brought your pizza to you. Now you're going to starve to death."

"My life is very complicated right now." Taking Dylan off speakerphone, I press my cell back to my ear, but the sound of a large vehicle pulling up outside and doors slamming pulls my attention away. Crossing my fingers, I press my lips to the phone. "I think help is here, talk later?"

"Let me know when you get your feet out, okay?" I swear I hear her laughing yet again as I'm hitting disconnect. That's what friends are for, right? Or maybe with friends like her I don't need enemies.

Heavy footsteps stomp up the sidewalk, up the front steps, and onto the porch, clomping all the way to the front door. A few short and sharp raps later, there's a tug on the locked door and they're banging at the entrance, the sound reverberating through my old farmhouse.

"Fire department! Maisey, can you let us in?"

I recognize the drawl of Dub, Dylan's dad. "I can't, but there is a key hidden on the porch. Under the green planter by the swing." An obvious nugget of info only given out on a need-to-know basis. Was I going to tell the pizza guy about that key? No. But Dubs? Not an issue.

A few moments later, Dubs throws my door open and shakes his head as he crosses the foyer and enters the living room.

"Connie said you were stuck in your foot massager, but I had to see it to believe it."

Pressing a hand to my hair, which I managed to gather and wrap up on the very top of my head into a neat bun—thank you very much—I flutter my eyelashes. "What can I say? I'm an attention seeker."

Dubs and two guys I only kind of know make their way into the room, all of them filling up the large space fairly quickly. These guys must work out a lot, because wow. Firemen everywhere.

Dubs eyes my Foot-Easy 3000. Tilting my chin in the general direction of the floor, I cross my arms across my chest. "What's the situation look like to you?"

The older man gives me his kindest smile. I've spent time

with Dubs as I've gotten to know Dylan, and he's become like a father to me. It's a sentiment I share with a lot of other folks in town, but I know my relationship with him is special because I'm so close to Dylan.

"I hate to say it, Maisey, but we're going to have to amputate." He waves a hand, getting the attention of one of the younger firefighters. "Can you run out and grab the Halligan for me?"

My stomach sinks. I paid over three hundred dollars for my fancy it's-a-treat-because-I-deserve-it massager and now it's headed to the chopping block. I guess this is why I can't have nice things.

I give Dubs my most pleading look, hoping against all hope he's messing with me. "Are you sure you have to break it open? Doesn't it have some bolts or something so it will pull apart?"

"I wish." Dubs slips off his helmet, his silver hair shining bright as the overhead lights in my living room cascade across it. "Sorry, Maisey. I know you love this thing."

"Like all things with love, it comes to a bitter, uneventful end." I wink at Dubs, playing up my moment of sarcasm. I'm relieved it's only him here and there's no Jack in sight. So there is no me having to deal with Jack McCoy. "And at the holidays, too, which is even more fitting."

"It's only the beginning of December, Maisey. There's still time for disappointment," Dubs clucks, winking. This is why I love this relationship; this man gets me. He plays my games with me and understands I'm not being serious when I pretend-whine about my relationship woes. Well, mostly. I might be half-serious about some of it.

"Touché." Looking across the room, I find one of the other firemen looking at the photos hanging on the wall of my family, moving awkwardly in his gear so he doesn't knock into anything. "By the way, I spoke to Dylan right before you got here and she said she's going home to work."

"She couldn't text me or write a note?" Dubs rolls his eyes.

Leaning back into my seat again, I shrug my shoulders. They're about the only part of me besides my hands and arms that's free to move. I wave a hand, Vanna White-style, in the direction of my foot prison. "Why do that when you have a hostage audience who can help and pass along a message?"

Dubs throws his head back and laughs, and as he does a familiar voice calls out from my porch. This particular voice has a gravely undertone mixed with a slight drawl and it blows one thousand tiny pieces of glass up and down my spine. It's irritating, like sand in your underwear unpleasant. As if I've been rolled around in butter and brown sugar and left out in the sunshine to bake at a hundred degrees. Nails on a chalkboard to my soul, I am telling you.

And yes, I have a flair for the dramatic. Sue me.

"Got the Halligan, Dubs." Blue eyes slam into mine as my nemesis comes into my sight. Watching him walk across my foyer, I start moving in the chair, suddenly twitchy. Having him here to witness me at my not-so-finest hour is really annoying, but it's gotta be done.

Never mind I used to have a crush on him. And never mind he asked me at my friend's wedding to go out on a date. And never mind that he never called.

Jack McCoy has entered the building.

CHAPTER 2

Jack

It's a good thing looks can't kill, because if they did I would have died a horrible death one thousand times over when I walked through the front door of Maisey Montgomery's farmhouse. I hoped I would have had a chance by now to talk to her and smooth things over since the last time we kind of spoke, but she's been avoiding me for months. The kind of avoidance that includes crossing the street when she sees me coming.

It's a small town so I knew eventually we'd be in the same room; I just never imagined she'd have to be held captive by a personal massager for it to happen, though.

"Hey, Maisey!" Two can play this game—I'll kill her with kindness. Throwing the Halligan over my shoulder, I stride into the foyer before heading into the living room where she sits, inclining my head in the direction of her feet. "That doesn't look like fun."

Her eyes, which have been boring a hole through mine, pull themselves away long enough to land on the massager at her feet. "Like most folks, I entered into my commitment with some expectations. Expectations which were let down, leaving me disappointed. Sound familiar?"

Dubs bites his bottom lip and turns his head away. I know this man well enough to know he's either uncomfortable or trying not to laugh. I think it's probably the former, but I'm going to pretend it's the latter.

"Well, thankfully it's only a massager and can be replaced." Go me. I'm going to keep it light and cheerful, 'cause there's a wall of dark and stormy headed my way and it's called Maisey.

Her emerald green eyes flash in my direction, watching my every move with keen interest as I kneel on the floor in front of her and position the bar to crack her massager open.

"That's the thing, Jack. When we have an expectation of something, or someone, it can be a huge bummer when you don't get what you 'pay for,' you know?"

Oh, I know. And I know exactly what she's talking about, too. Hurricane Maisey seems to be growing in size, perhaps puffing up to scare me—and it's working.

"Well," Dubs says after he clears his throat. "It's a good thing we always get what we pay for when we go to the Red Bird. Your food is the best, Maisey. Right, McCoy?" Bending at the waist, he holds on tightly to the massager, stabilizing it for me, and gives me a knowing look as he changes the subject. "You know, Maisey, your mom would be really proud of what you've done with the place since you took it over."

"Thanks, Dubs, that makes me happy to hear." Maisey's eyes drift to a photo sitting on her fireplace mantel. I recognize a young teenaged Maisey in the photo standing with her arm wrapped around her mother in front of a Christmas tree. "This time of year she comes to mind every day."

"She was a maniac for Christmas," the old guy says with a chuckle. "She was the kind of woman who played Christmas carols in October. Made me nuts, but she got a kick out of it."

Maisey's features soften, her lips slowly curl upwards. "It

brought her great delight to have Christmas tunes on when it was Halloween."

"I hate to butt in, but I can free you now." I hand Maisey a thick blanket I brought in with me from the truck. "Throw this over your body and cover your face, in case any shards fly up. Dubs, keep that thing still."

It only takes one smack of the Halligan tool to crack the massager into seven chunks of plastic and machinery, all of which disperse in a circular array around us. Dubs and I each hold out a hand to Maisey at the same time, intending to help her stand up. No surprise here when she opts for Dubs' hand over mine.

"Thank you," she murmurs, wrapping her arms around the big guy and giving him a hug. "I owe you one. Next meal is on me."

"All in a day's work." Dubs waves at the other two firemen standing in the hallway, and the trio head out the door. "See you soon, Maisey."

"How about the rest of us?" I'm kidding, but Maisey doesn't care. She finishes waving goodbye to Dubs before she spins around on one foot and stares me down. It's back...that look that could sink a thousand ships is there again, and I can tell I'm being un-alived all over the place in her mind.

She walks over to her front door and holds it wide open. "You came, you fixed things. Thank you." Maisey clasps her hands together in front of her, plastering a fake smile on that gorgeous face of hers. "Well, you know what they say. Y'all come back now...ya hear? Unless you're not invited."

This woman can hold a grudge. That she's so mad at me doesn't eliminate the fact I've had a crush on her since I moved to town.

And I kind of deserve it.

Kind of.

I walk out the door, turning back around when both feet

are on the hardwood of her front porch. Maisey's hair is pulled back into a bun and she's wearing a sweatshirt with stains down the front of it. She's also limping, the result of her feet being cramped in the tiny cave of her foot massager for a few hours.

She's absolutely stunning.

"You say I'm not invited, but I made it inside tonight." I wink, pretty sure I can elicit one smile before we go.

"I'd have let a vampire in tonight, Jack, as long as he promised he would help me get out of that bear trap I was stuck in. So, thanks. Have a good night," she calls out as she steps back and slams the door shut in my face.

Making my way back to the fire truck, three blank expressions wait to greet me. Scratch that. Two blank expressions and one that's lit up with glee, because Dubs loves watching when someone gives me grief.

"You've gone and done it, and you've gone and done it real good, haven't you?" Dubs chuckles as he turns the key and gets the engine revved up. Sitting stick-straight in the driver's seat, he turns to face me, shaking his head. "That woman is mad at you."

Crossing my arms over my chest, I try my sternest expression on for size and stare right back at him. "I've not done anything I can't explain or fix."

Dubs points to the house. "She's furious. You know she's friends with my daughter, right?"

"Of course I do. Dylan talks about hanging out with her all the time."

"Yep." Throwing the gear into drive, he navigates the large truck down the bumpy country lane. "So, I know you asked Maisey out. I know you made a date, canceled it at the last minute, and never followed up."

Man. Being a dude, I forget women talk.

A lot. And to each other.

"Yeah." Sliding my helmet off my head, I place it on the floor at my feet. "I did do that, but..."

"There are no buts in small-town dating, my friend," Dubs says with a cackle as he turns out onto the main road, pointing the truck in the direction of town. "Do yourself a favor and stop by the cafe this week and tell her, properly, that you're sorry."

"Can't I defend myself here? I have a good reason, a very good one at that, for why I couldn't go out with her."

"I'm not the one who needs to hear it." He jerks a thumb over his shoulder in the general direction of where we'd just come from. "She does."

He's right. Of course he's right; the guy's been around the block a few times. Married three times himself, with an amazing daughter who teaches him to be a better man every day (or so she says).

Maisey does deserve an apology. I want to explain to her why I canceled, why I called at the literal eleventh hour to back out of our date without any real explanation except that I wasn't going to make it. I never promised I'd call again, even though I meant to—and tonight, I witnessed first-hand how mad she really is at me.

Sighing, I throw my head back onto the seat of the truck, closing my eyes. The last year of my life hasn't been an easy one; something had to give. I'm processing the fact that maybe it's me when we pull into the bay of the firehouse, back at last and hopefully in for the night.

We clear out the rig quickly, and I'm climbing the stairs to my office to wrap up paperwork when my cell phone dings in my pocket. Seeing my mom's name flashing on the screen, I grin and tap the button immediately to say hello.

"Is this my son who has not given me any grandchildren to spoil yet?" My mother's guilting talent is on a level that can only be equated to that of an Olympic athlete. Fine-tuned and perfected skills, they are.

"I didn't even get to say hello this time." She's on a mission. I'm the youngest of three and the only one who hasn't settled down. Let me rephrase: I've not settled down the way my family, and my mother, expects me to. Hmm. There sure are a lot of lessons in expectations coming up for me tonight.

"Hello, my sweet Jack. How have things been?" Her Southern drawl is as thick as one of Maisey's milkshakes. "Is it as cold in North Carolina as it is here in D.C.?"

My mom is originally from Lake Lorelei, only leaving to move to New York City with my father when he'd been selected for a prestigious position with one of New York's busiest firehouses. We lived there, quite happily, until he passed away after a long battle with cancer. My mother was so overcome with grief, she'd asked her job to transfer her anywhere they had a position open at the time—so we ended up in Washington D.C.

"Things are good, except I need to know what Grandmom wants me to bring to her place for Christmas Eve. Has she given you a list yet?"

"You could bring a girlfriend!" is the response someone screams in my ear. Looks like I'm on speakerphone.

"Hi, Gran. Didn't know you were visiting Mom." Now, this woman is like an elderly tornado. She's in her eighties, plays bingo here at the fire hall once a week, goes to church every Sunday, and is still in charge of writing the newsletter for her local club. I think it's the Daughters of the American Revolution, but to be honest, I can't keep up. "When did you land in D.C.?"

"She came up yesterday," Mom chimes in. "And we'll all be flying back together next week in enough time to get her place ready for the big party. Will you be staying with us on Christmas Eve this year?"

"Depends on how the schedule shakes out, but I'm going to give the guys who have families off that day, or at least give some of them the morning off." Just because I don't have a family of my own, doesn't mean I can't relate.

The audible sigh I expect slams against my ear and then some. Pretty sure Mom adds an extra "aaahhhh" to the end of this one, drawing out the syllable as long as a giraffe's neck. I can just picture my mother leaning over into the phone to breathe heavily on purpose, simply so I can feel and truly know her displeasure. "I hate we have to share you like this, but I love that you're a first responder. So, I can't stay mad."

"Thanks. When I save a family from a burning building I'll let them know my mommy has approved of my job," I tease.

"Shut it, Jack. Be nice to Mom, it's Christmas."

Now, there's a voice that makes me happy.

"You're there, too, Ets?" My twin sister, Etta. She has the power to both lift me up and tear me down in one fell swoop. She's the oldest of the two of us, born about ten minutes before I was and yes, I do love to remind her she's older. But she loves to remind me I'm the baby.

"Stopped by for coffee, and apparently I'm about to take these two out shopping for the last of their Christmas gifts."

"Good luck with that, I'm sure..."

The phone sounds like it's been dropped—there's clanking and a few beeps before I realize I've been taken off speakerphone and Etta's in my ear all by herself now.

"Jack." Her whisper is like a stage mom hiding behind a curtain at their ten-year-old's first play. It's nearly non-existent. "These two have been moaning all morning about you."

She's also a bit dramatic.

"What do you mean?"

"Mom started with the 'he's not even dating' and then Gran encourages her, tells her she knows some lovely young ladies in Lake Lorelei she could introduce you to. Jack, listen to me. You do not want that. I've seen pictures, and they're not your type."

Etta must have pressed her lips right up to the receiver to whisper that last sentence—I swear, there's spit in my ear canal.

"You're being overdramatic."

"Ha!" A whoosh of air hits my ear as she exhales a huge huff. "You know how they just said they're coming in a week early to help set up? They're coming in early to try and arrange a date for you with one of Gran's friend's daughters who's in town for the holidays next weekend. So, be warned. Mom's seriously looking for you to bring an actual date with you this year, or she's going to stick you in a bachelor auction. Mark my words, man!"

"Don't you worry. I can handle them." At least I hope I can. I already know I won't be showing up to the party with a date, unless a small miracle happens. "I'll let Mom know if she pushes me too much I may leave her grandchildless for life. And Gran can kiss my Sunday dinners at her place goodbye if she keeps this up."

"Wow. I figured you'd be mildly irritated with these two, not so much wanting revenge," she manages through fits of laughter. "But, if you threaten Gran with barring her from the bingo hall..."

"She'd kill me. Like the time I kicked over Auntie Mabel's chewing can, she was furious. Remember that?"

Judging from the laughter on the other end, Etta knows exactly what I mean. My Auntie Mabel was the epitome of a tough, old Southern woman. She had a hard but quite colorful life, and over the years she had picked up some interesting habits. One of them was her love of chewing tobacco.

I can remember our mother preparing for Auntie Mabel's visits—we always had to have an empty coffee can ready for when she arrived because she needed somewhere to spit her chew, thank you very much.

Auntie Mabel kept that coffee can at her feet at all times, and just because it was Christmas didn't mean the can was off for the holidays. No siree. Every Christmas morning, as we were all gathered in the living room, tearing open presents and running around, Auntie Mabel would have her can set out next to her armchair.

But one Christmas morning, I didn't see it.

In the middle of a game of Christmas wrapping-paper-basketball (Mom's made-up game so we'd help clean up faster) I moved to intercept a piece of glittery paper Etta tossed, only I wasn't paying attention. My foot connected with the old coffee can, sending it flying and rotating, slowly, emptying its contents all over us, our new gifts, and Gran's house as it launched across the room, landing upside down in my mother's lap. Eat that, David Beckham.

"I'm still not sure why we got in trouble." Etta takes a deep breath, trying to slow her giggles down. My sis can be a very serious person, but her one tick is that she giggles at the most inopportune times. Of course, she does it when she's happy, like now, but it sometimes happens when she's anxious or when she's backed in a corner, thus causing anxiety so cue the giggle fit. "Liam was the one who was egging us on that day, hyping us up so we were more excited than usual."

"I'm sure Gran's party will be a blast this year, like it always is. If I don't bring a date, it means I can spend more time with you and take care of Liam's little ones. I'll even take your dogs for a walk. Give you guys a break, right?"

"You know," Etta says, her voice going soft, "they just want you to be happy."

"You know," I retort, "those two nosey Rosie's can mind

their own business."

"They won't." In the background there's a clamor and a bang, making it clear there's something going on. Etta growls. "Okay, so Mom's trying to get a suitcase down with Gran's help. Those lovely ladies just chucked their suitcases over the banister onto the second floor."

I've witnessed this kind of obstinate coordination from these two before. "You should go, it sounds like you're herding cats over there."

"Babysitting toddlers, more like it. Talk later."

I tap end on the screen, then toss the phone onto the desk beside me so I can think.

A date for my family's holiday party. Dating. A date for Christmas.

Sitting back in my desk chair, I kick my feet up onto my desk. Clasping my hands behind my head, I lean all the way back in my chair, sinking into the headrest so I can stare at the ceiling above. My mother means well; she wants me to be happy. To have companionship, and romance, and all of that jazz. And you know what? I want it too, only I think I know who I want it with—and I think I screwed it up.

There's this woman here in town I used to be friendly with. She's funny and charming, and there's a heat that flushes through my body as soon as I hear her name or see her standing in front of me.

She's been so preoccupied with being irritated with me that I don't think she's noticed how I show up at her work at least once a day when I'm on my shift for a cup of coffee or for a piece of her homemade pie—and I'm not even a big fan of sweets. When I'm off work I still manage to go by her cafe. I'm a single man who likes takeout, so placing an order for a barbeque pork platter from the Red Bird once a week isn't that big a deal.

And it gives me a chance to see Maisey.

CHAPTER 3

Maisey

"Order up for a crab cake platter, a barbeque pork sandwich, and two sides of coleslaw. Can someone run this to the dining room?"

My head chef, Craig, barks orders from behind the kitchen line at the same time I hip-check the swinging kitchen door, opening it and strutting into the back of the house. Yes, I strut, because it's Friday night and the cafe is full. Holiday shopping always brings in plenty of business, and thank goodness we're prepared.

"I've got it." Standing at the counter, I throw him a mock salute. "Your runner is here, present and accounted for, sir."

"Thanks, Maisey." Peering in between the stainless steel shelves, Craig repositions his favorite baseball hat (Baltimore Orioles. He's been a fan FOREVER) so his bangs are out of his eyes before he points to the plates under the heat lamps. "They went up a few seconds ago, so if you could take them out now, it'd be a big help."

There's already a tray set up on the counter, making it even easier for me to slide the dinner plates onto the waiting transportation and run them out to the dining room.

Weaving around the tables on my way to drop off the goods, I make sure to double-check everyone has full drinks—it's my pet peeve. I impress this habit on my front of house staff, too. We do *not* let our customers' drinks get less than halfway down without a refill. My other golden rule at the Red Bird is to always clear all used plates immediately, whether it's your table or not. No one needs to sit during their meal-time with dirty dishes on their table. No one.

The place is packed tonight. We have a waiting list at the hostess stand and a line out the door, yet everything is running smoothly. One of the servers took it upon themselves to pass out hors d'oeuvres to the folks who are waiting for their tables, and the chairs in the lobby are filled with happy, smiling guests. There's a general hum of activity and an undercurrent of happiness in the restaurant and it thrills me. Mom would have been so proud.

I drop off the food and walk over to the hostess station to find the waitlist is finally thinning out—we're turning over tables quickly tonight. A cold blast of air hits me as the front door swings open. Out of reflex I grab a couple of menus, ready to do my usual warm "Welcome to the Red Bird!" spiel, but it's only Dylan so I chuck the menus back onto the stand. If anyone knows the food we serve by heart, it would be her. She's here almost every other day—not that I'm complaining.

Grinning at my friend, I pull her in for a quick hug. "Are you here for food or company tonight?"

Dylan's face screws up, but laughter dances in her eyes. She chews on her bottom lip anxiously, like it's a piece of bubble gum.

"Okay, you're either the cat who ate the canary, or you know where the canary is being held and you're here to broker the kidnapping fee." She tries to slide past me, but I cross my arms in front of my chest and block her path. "What's up?"

Dylan cocks her head to one side and narrows her eyes,

wagging a finger in the air. "Did you enter that essay contest I told you about last week?"

"The one for the Mistletoe Lodge?"

A tiny shadow flickers across Dylan's features, and her eyes narrow even further. She looks like a snake...the snake that ate the canary.

"That's the one." She steps closer to me, dropping the volume of her voice a notch. It's as close to a hiss as one can get in a loud cafe. "Did you enter it?"

"Well, yes." This inquisition is making me nervous. Dylan knows my anxiety can be off the charts, and being cornered at the front of my restaurant, and at the end of the dinner rush, isn't helping. "I entered twice, I think. But I'm not sure."

"You entered twice?" Dylan slowly nods her head, punctuating each word and scratching her chin at the same time. She reminds me of a sleuth. Not Nancy Drew, more Miss Marple, maybe. "What do you mean you entered twice?"

"Well, if you must know, I wrote my first essay being really silly. I made up a fiancé and told them this epic love story about how we met. I wrote that we worked together years ago before I had to leave the job, but we ran into each other again last year when he helped me change a flat tire when I was stuck on the side of the road. The rest is engagement history." I hold up a hand, correcting myself. "Well, fake engagement history."

"You did what now?" she asks before slapping her hand to her mouth in surprise, her eyes growing even wider than before. All of this reaction injects a shockwave of worry into my heart.

"Dylan, you're freaking me out." A bead of sweat forms on my brow and it's not from the heater being turned up too high in the cafe. "What are you getting at here?"

"Oh, you wait." Dylan holds one of her hands up, stopping me in my proverbial tracks. "We'll get there. So what did you do after you wrote the first essay?"

"I threw it away." Somewhere in the busy space, a rousing chorus of "Happy Birthday" begins, while at the hostess station, I can hear the funeral march on repeat in my head. "I'm pretty sure I deleted it, rewrote my essay, and gave them a love story that is true. It's my love story with the Red Bird."

Dylan squares her shoulders, crossing her arms in front of her chest. "Uh huh."

"Don't do that." She knows that kind of vague answer only makes me more anxious. "That's a loaded 'uh huh.'"

"Well, I'm here to let you know that the Mistletoe Lodge announced the winner of their giveaway today." Dylan hands me her phone. "Looks like you and your fiancé are going to have a blast."

A rush of ice-cold water hits my veins. Dylan holds her phone out to me and I can only stare at it.

"Go on," she encourages me, shoving the phone under my nose. "See what you've done."

I snatch the phone from Dylan's outstretched hand and stare at the screen. My stomach hits the floor at the same time my jaw goes slack when I see what's waiting for my viewing pleasure.

On the screen is a photo of my smiling face, taken the other night in front of my Christmas tree while I wrote my essay. Well, essays if we're going to get technical. I sat down and wrote my first essay, the one where I made up my perfect man.

That was my fake essay. One I wrote to be ridiculous. Did I insert a little bit of wishful thinking into it as well? You bet, I was on a roll so I made it good. Did I change my mind when it was done and hit the delete button? Yes...at least I think I did? Come to think of it, the delete button and the submit button were a little close together. Maybe I did enter by accident...

But I won.

Next to me, Dylan shakes with laughter. "Are you proud of yourself?"

"Looks like I should be, since I've won a romantic getaway for two to a local resort." I grab the stack of menus again, placing them in front of me as I swipe a rag from under the counter to wipe them down, even though I'm still clutching her phone. You know, I want to look busy and all that. "And what, pray tell, have you done today?"

"Maisey, I need you to be serious." Dylan claws the phone back from my grip, pointing at the screen. "Did you read what the post says? "We're thrilled to welcome Miss Montgomery *with her fiancé* to the Mistletoe Lodge for the weekend of their Christmas dreams." Did you know that you'd have to take your fiancé with you?"

Did I think this through? Obviously, no.

Did I know I entered myself and my fake fiancé into the contest? Definitely not.

"Of course I did not know that, Dylan." I toss the rag onto the counter, too flustered to wipe anything "I didn't plan on winning."

She's still laughing and it's not helpful. I may scream. No, I'm going to scream and run out the door.

"Maisey." Dylan's voice is steady, and even though her mouth quirks while fighting back a laugh, her demeanor is serious. She places her hand on my arm. "The fine print says you need to be coming with your partner. A fiancé."

"An easy fix." I shrug. "You come with me. We'll have a girls' weekend and I'll say you're my fiancé."

"As tempting as it is, I can't." Dylan, still holding the phone out like it's her tiny chalkboard to point to, runs her finger under a line of text. "See this paragraph? 'Miss Montgomery's essay introduced us to her fiancé who is also her very own larger than life hero. Not only does *he* work with a charity for rehoming dogs on the weekends, but he spends his time in his community helping those around him who are less fortunate. He's the kind of man who has mastered the art of listening, has no issues with doing the laundry, and supports her every move. The staff here at the Mistletoe Lodge cannot wait to welcome the two of you with open arms.'"

I feel like Dylan is making way more out of this than it needs to be. "I'm not seeing the problem."

"I can't go with you because they know your fiancé is a man, okay? So they'll be expecting you to show up with this man-hero-laundry-doer-and-charity-worker you've written about. He must be ab-so-loving-lutely amazing because they cannot wait to meet him."

Okay, am I freaked out? Yes. But it's going to be okay... because I have an idea.

"Fine, he'll get sick and won't be able to make it. I'll tell them the day I arrive—or rather, we arrive."

Dylan shakes her head. "Not going to work. Ts and Cs, Maisey."

Groaning, I grab the phone back and go to their website to look at the terms and conditions of entry, something I should have paid attention to the other night.

Groaning won't even help me now. It's all written, right there in the fine print. "'The winners must be available for the weekend dates reserved for the contest or they forfeit any rights.' Oh, boy. This is ironclad, isn't it?"

Tears silently streaming down her cheeks, Dylan doubles over with one hand gripping the hostess desk. "Oh, it gets better."

"I don't understand this. I don't remember sending in the essay about having a fiancé; I decided to send in the one I wrote about how much I love the Red Bird and how it means so much to me. I wrote my love story about the cafe, the fact Mom gave it to me, and that she is the one who had a strong connection to the Mistletoe."

"Obviously, one of them didn't make it through." She snickers while smoothing her hair back out of her face. "Or, you deleted the wrong entry, my sweet technology-repelling friend."

I'm officially entering grumble mode. "You said this gets better, so I can only assume that's your sarcastic way of letting me know it's about to get much worse?"

A round of mildly hysterical laughter answers my query.

"Fine." I sigh, gripping the tiny cell phone tighter in my hand. I hold it so tight I could squeeze it right now and make it pop. "Hit me with it. What else?"

She leans over my shoulder and thumbs the screen, scrolling to show me what I've agreed to do. She points to what I can only assume is, again, more fine print I really should have paid attention to the other night.

"You and your fiancé will be interviewed by their public relations team for content they can use across their holiday and wedding venue marketing plans. This part"—she points to a list of items—"tells you what clothes to bring and they even suggest colors, because you'll have a photographer around, snapping photos of the two of you having your romantic getaway and taking part in some of their experiences on the estate."

"What the—" My stomach flips. I'm sick, like I drank a gallon of grease. "I only want to go to the museum and walk around, have a day to sleep in, maybe be spoiled just a little. I don't want to go on a flipping walkabout."

"Walkabout? I don't know where you come up with those sayings." Dylan snickers, shaking her head. "But they're the best. We need a book for them."

Rolling my eyes, I playfully swat at her arm. "Come back to the part where we're followed by a camera guy?"

"Staff photographer. Who is possibly also their social

media manager. Apparently, they'll be using these photos for the next few years when they do holiday marketing."

The tiny pit which had started forming when the conversation began just opened up.

Wide. Grand Canyon-gaping-hole wide.

I fight the urge to shriek. "You've got to be kidding me!"

"No, I'm not," she manages as she gives in to a fit of giggles once again.

"You're evil." I throw a towel at Dylan's head and sit down limply on a bar stool, resting

my elbows on the counter. "I have no idea what to do. Maybe I can talk Reid into going with me."

Reid's another local fireman, and he's my friend Ari's brother. I'm searching my memory banks and I'm pretty sure he owes me a favor.

"I know for a fact he's not here that weekend. He's in Beaufort, South Carolina for yearly training. You've been on that dating app, Dinner Dates, for months. There's no one there you're interested in?"

"Please. That app was used once to set up my account, that's all." Maybe I swiped it a few times, but never went on any dates. Not my thing.

Dylan raises an eyebrow when she looks at me. "I'm going to throw a random thought out there. Maybe you call the Mistletoe Lodge and say you can't make it, avoid all of this madness. Just simply don't go."

Is she right? Of course she is, but I like winning. Scratch that. I LOVE it. I'm competitive by nature, and now that I know I won this, I have to have it. But, I really do have my own reasons for wanting to get to the Mistletoe Lodge this year, and I want to see this through. "I can't admit defeat, now can I?"

"Admit you messed up. Send them the other essay and explain what happened."

"I could ignore all of this." I shrug a shoulder. "Play dumb."

Dylan throws her hands in the air. "You're not dumb."

"Please. I know this." Do I scoff? You bet, I'm scoffing. Whatever that is.

"But you messed up."

"I did. But I did it with love in my heart and for the right reasons." We sit in silence for a few minutes with the sounds of the cafe around us.

Do I think I should have won with my fake essay? No, but it doesn't change the fact I get to go now. I may be acting out of character, but this Christmas I'm really missing my mother and the Mistletoe Lodge was one of those holiday traditions we used to do together—until I stopped coming home.

My mother was so committed to going every year, she would start planning our day there months in advance. It always surprised my sister and I how many people she knew when we would visit, but she'd been going for years, always at the same time of year. Always Christmas—and we'd always go see the art exhibit.

She was so obsessed with their art exhibits and gallery, she was even invited to a special holiday reception for their patrons a few years ago. I never understood why she got the invitation —because she wasn't a patron, per se—but she never made it. It was the year her Alzheimer's took over and life as we knew it changed. We had boxed up the invitation with some of her things and I hadn't thought about it since.

Then, this year, I grabbed the wrong box from the attic when I pulled out the holiday decorations. When I opened the one labeled "Christmas garland," a pile of old paperwork fell out along with some of my mom's mail and old letters. The formal invitation from the Mistletoe Lodge had fluttered its way to the ground, landing at my feet and reigniting the unanswered question from years ago.

I tried calling to see if anyone at the lodge could tell me why she had been sent the invite, but no one there had an answer for me. The docent didn't have any records of her on file for donations or volunteer work, and when I spoke to the administrative offices they, too, were stumped.

Snapping out of my daze, I look around the cafe. Tables are clearing out, signaling the rush is over. And I'm coming to a realization that maybe Dylan is right. My wanting to go to the Mistletoe Lodge is the result of my connection to my mother. I told a story with my story, and it doesn't matter if it's the winner, now I need to make it right.

I shift from one foot to the other, facing Dylan as I pull my cell phone out of my back pocket. "I'm going to call them tomorrow first thing and let them know I can't do it."

"Good, that sounds sane." She swipes her phone off the hostess station and slides it in her pocket. "I gotta run, I've got paramedic training in the morning. When you call the Mistletoe Lodge, try telling them about your other essay. Maybe even email it first so they can read it before you call, but hop on it fast so you don't get pulled in deeper than you already are."

"Deeper?" My turn to laugh 'cause I feel like I'm pulling myself out of a bog of quicksand. "I don't think it can get deeper than it already has, but I hear you."

After assuring Dylan at least two more times I'll take care of it, she finally leaves. The cafe is quiet, the dinner rush is officially now over. I grab a bus tub and start clearing off tables to help my staff.

Heading toward the front of the cafe, I set up at a row of tables positioned by the main window, where there's a direct view across the street and over to the fire station. Funny that, how things you've never noticed before suddenly pop up when you focus your attention there. Like the way my eyes flick to a window on the second floor of the firehouse at this very moment. I make out Jack's silhouette, his hands moving in the air around him like he's talking to someone. It's not that I'm being super creepy or anything. It's the main street, so it's not like I'm crawling around a back alley trying to peer in his windows.

I've got enough to worry about anyway, right now. I do not need to worry about Jack McCoy. Never mind he's ridiculously handsome and I used to have a crush on him. Forget the fact he's probably the town's most eligible bachelor and he did ask me out once. He also canceled and never called again like he said he was going to do.

Instead, I had the luxury of witnessing him a week later hugging some gorgeous redhead—and really tightly, too—in front of the firehouse. I could have written it off, but when the same woman showed up again a few more times in town, always with him—I took the hint.

So, yeah. Never mind Jack "I'm-a-fireman-and-can-save-your-life" McCoy with his kind eyes and broad shoulders.

Never you mind.

Because I kind of don't like him now.

CHAPTER 4

Jack

Is it weird that I'm spending my morning staring out the window of my office at the cafe across the street, wondering if I can go back in for yet another piece of pie today? You'd think I'd be full since I managed to eat my weight in breakfast. I've had one omelet, a side of bacon, a fruit cup, two slices of today's pie —strawberry rhubarb, yum—and I've sucked down two lattes. I've gone over to the Red Bird at least three times already today to get takeout for "the guys," but the thing is…I'm not sharing.

I'm trying to think of any excuse I can to see Maisey, that's what I'm doing. She wasn't there the first two times I went over, but she was back in the kitchen when I went over the third time. I've seen her through the window, walking around the main dining room, and chatting with customers sitting at the tables.

Gripping my fourth coffee of the day, I shakily hold it in one hand while using the other to keep me propped in the right position to spy on the Red Bird from my window. I want to go over and say I'm sorry, but it needs to be at the right moment, so technically me peering out my window and watching Maisey isn't *that* crazy. It's reconnaissance for a greater good.

Someone clears their throat behind me. "Something interesting happening on Main Street?"

Spinning around, I find Dylan leaning on my doorjamb with her arms crossed in front of her chest.

"No, just thinking." Yes, I'm lying, but I don't need Maisey's best friend to know what I'm doing. My cheeks flush with traitorous heat. "What's up, Dylan?"

"Looking for my dad. Is he around?"

"In the kitchen." I head out the door, leading us down the hall to the joint lounge and kitchen space. Dubs is right where I thought he'd be—at the dining table pouring over today's newspaper.

"Thanks," Dylan says, patting my arm. She skips over to the table, joining her father and Reid, one of our full-time firemen. I grab a glass from the cabinet with the intention to get water in my body to help move all this caffeine through me. Stay hydrated and get back into my office, because there is actual work I need to do today.

However, the room I'm in is only so big. Sometimes you can't help but eavesdrop, and I've learned when Reid Shannon starts laughing like a hyena with hiccups, you stick around to find out what the reason is.

"Seriously? I'm glad you told her I can't go." Reid shakes his head, his eyes darting back and forth between Dylan and Dubs. "I'm not even around that weekend and now I'm grateful."

"I told her that, Reid, and I told her you weren't allowed to go, either," Dylan says as she pats his back. "She's a woman unhinged. She tried to get me to go, too."

"That's hilarious," Dubs says, laughing. Picking up his glass of iced tea, he spins it in a circle, watching the ice cubes go round and round. "Okay, how did Maisey win a weekend for two to the Mistletoe Lodge?"

My ears perk up and suddenly filling this glass of water is taking as long as it takes to build a bridge.

"I told her about the essay contest they were doing," Dylan says with a shrug. "She says she accidentally entered twice, one story was real and the other one not so much…guess which story made it through and won?"

Dubs groans. "The fake one?"

"Yep. She made up a fiancé, won the trip away, and now she's refusing to let it go."

Before I can stop myself, I jump into the middle of their conversation. "Why?"

Dylan turns around in her chair to face me, cocking her head to one side. "Are you butting in here?"

I sweep my hands around the small room. "It's not like you're whispering. Why is she so determined to go on this trip?"

"I don't know. Why do birds fly?" Dylan throws a hand in the air. "She's on a mission to go to the Mistletoe Lodge this year. She's got some connection with it because of her mom."

"She can't go on her own, another time?" Reid points out. "Does it have to be Christmas?"

Dylan shrugs again, this time shaking her head. "I don't know. I do know that while my friend has woven herself into a problem that is huge, she is going to be sad if she can't go. She was really excited to see the winners will be treated to a private tour of the Mistletoe's art collection."

"She can go see art in Charlotte. What's so impressive about the Mistletoe?" Reid asks.

"Even though it used to be a full-time art gallery, the Mistletoe Lodge only opens the floor housing their personal art pieces as an exhibit once a year." Tipping my water glass in

Dylan's direction, I punctuate this fact. "And, it's always at Christmas."

"Thus, her conundrum." Dylan sighs, tapping the table. "I wish I could rent a fiancé for her to take this weekend."

"Now, I'd go if she paid me..." Reid's joking, but the words no sooner leave his lips before Dubs smacks the back of his head.

Am I thinking about how much I wish I could go swooping in right now and volunteer for this role? Yes, one hundred percent I am. I also know an offer like that coming from me is not going to be taken well. In no fantasy world of any kind do I think Maisey is waiting for me to be her real-life knight in shining armor. That ship has sailed. Well, it's stuck on the rocks, at least.

The vibration of my phone snaps me back to the present. Swiping it from my pocket, I see it's Etta calling for the fourth time in two days. Holidays. They stress everyone out.

"Hey, sis, what now? Do I need to pick up some gluten free bread for you?"

"Keep your voice down." She exhales a sigh so loud, it's like a wind tunnel in my ear. "They'll know I'm talking to you."

"Okay." I can be vague sometimes, but at this moment, Etta takes the cake. I lower my voice to her same conspiratorial level. "And who are 'they?'"

"Mom and Gran."

"What did they do now?"

"Did they tell you about this dinner they're planning this weekend when they get back to town?"

I vaguely remember a text coming through in the last few days, letting me know I was expected to be at dinner on Saturday. "They did."

Etta scoffs. "Well, this Saturday night's guest list includes a few of Gran's friends coming around."

"That sounds like it'll be nice." And unassuming. I'm not sure what the issue is. "Good for Gran and Mom, too."

"But this is not good for you. The guest list includes at least three eligible women, granddaughters of Gran's old friends. These two women are planning to give you your own speed dating event, and all from the comfort of your grandmother's home. Ho, ho, ho. Merry Christmas."

My jaw hits the floor. "You have got to be kidding me."

"It's Mom. She thinks she's being helpful."

My head starts thumping. "This stresses me out."

"I figured it would. I'm telling you, you should just tell them you have a girlfriend to shut them down." Etta feels my pain, but only to some degree. While my mom and grandmother love to give me the full court press to settle down, they leave her alone for now because of her job. She's so busy running her own winery that Mom considers that her relationship. For now. But me? I need to front up and get married, like my big brother, Liam. "Maybe you can go away this weekend. Isn't there something you can be busy doing or a friend you can go visit?"

Racking my brain, I can think of no one. A couple of the guys I know fairly well from the firehouse are out of town this weekend doing annual training, and Dubs' place is crowded with him and Dylan living there, so I can't hide there. I've got some old friends who live just outside of town, but they're out of the country until next year.

Walking back into my office, I perch on the window ledge and stare out across Main Street. I'm going down a list of excuses I can use with Etta when a flash of red movement catches my eye.

Dragging my eyes north, I spy Maisey Montgomery outside her restaurant setting up a ladder with one of her employees beside her. Judging from the box at her feet, they're about to hang Christmas lights. Chewing on my lip, my tummy hitches.

I've got an idea.

Across the street is a woman in need and she just so happens to be the exact same person I need to speak to right now—whether she likes it or not.

* * *

Lake Lorelei's Main Street is one of the prettiest places to be at the holidays. It's got that typical small-town Americana charm happening, where all of the store owners go all out for holidays like Christmas, Halloween, and Easter. It's the Christmas holiday that's my personal favorite, and it's all thanks to my dad.

We were the family that jumped in our car every Christmas season and made a whole night out driving around the neighborhood to see how folks decorated their homes. Some of the smaller boroughs in the city had contests, and since my dad was a fireman we had the inside scoop on the best parts of New York for our viewing pleasure.

Lake Lorelei does something similar to those old New York neighborhoods where they go all out and put on a show for the community. They even have a contest for the best shop front and window dressing every year. Judging by the amount of Christmas lights, faux snow flocking, and mistletoe strewn on the sidewalk at her feet, today's the day Maisey's setting up the Red Bird's window for their entry.

As I cross the street, Maisey's voice rises above the hustle and bustle of the cars going by and it brings a nervous warmth to my gut.

"Craig, if you can pass me that end of the lights, I'll get up on the ladder and secure them with the gutter hooks, cool?"

She stands with her back to me, pointing to show Craig

where she wants to string the lights, head cocked to one side to keep the sun from shining in her eyes. The way the morning light falls around her, Maisey literally glows, and per usual, she takes my breath away. The way her hand rests on her hip draws my eye to her curves, but I stop myself from thinking anything more. I have a mission to complete.

In the time it takes me to walk up to them, Maisey's already scrambled to the top of the ladder. She turns around, rolling her eyes as soon as she notices me walking up behind Craig.

"Hey, Jack," Craig calls out when he sees me. "Nice morning, huh?"

"Sure is. " Inclining my head in Craig's direction, I keep my eyes trained on Maisey. "Maisey, you okay up there?"

The way her hackles raise when I check on her wellbeing... I should have known not to ask this woman if she's okay.

"I'm perfectly capable of hanging some lights up without the help of the local fire department, but thanks anyway," she sings out. A song laced with sarcasm, but she isn't totally unpleasant. We're making progress.

Craig's phone beeps. He reads the screen and immediately tilts his head up the ladder to Maisey.

"Hey, I gotta go, boss. I forgot I had to pick up our meat order this week." Turning his head to the side, he throws me a wink. "The delivery girl's truck broke down, so I have to pick it up from her."

"Really. Now?" Maisey peers down at us, her face registering disappointment. She considers his request for a second before sitting on the top of the ladder and throwing her hands in the air. "Do what you gotta do, but how soon do you think you'll be back? We really need to get this part of the holiday decorations done today. Christmas will be over by the time we're looking celebratory."

Craig shakes his head. "Not sure. Back within the next two hours, I suppose."

Maisey's shoulders hike next to her ears, prompting me to raise my hand.

"I can help." Pointing to the assortment of holiday decorations at his feet, I exchange a knowing look with Craig. "We do this to the firehouse, too, you guys. I'm here and happy to give Maisey a hand so you can go get your order."

"I do not want to take up your precious..." Maisey begins to say, but Craig's already one foot off the sidewalk.

"Thank you! Jack, I owe you one." He waves to Maisey, who shoots him that look that could kill a man. "Maisey, I'll make it back in record time. I promise."

Craig pulls his keys out of his pocket and pats me on the back before taking off down the street toward his car. Lifting my head, I cover my eyes to shield the sun and grin.

"Looks like I'm your assistant now."

Maisey looks at me like I have twelve heads floating in the air around me. Her lips snarl in a way one can only compare to something seen in a wildlife documentary. I can hear the voice-over now: "The female polar bear put the male polar bear in her sights and he was never seen again."

"I don't need your help, Jack." Green eyes flash with irritation and it's aimed right at me. Luckily, I've got my bullet-proof shield on.

"Since I work for the community, it's my duty to help residents in a time of crisis." Stepping back, I wave my arms out wide and point to the front of the Red Bird. "I'm here to help. Here to help you, oh community member and resident. Where do I start?"

I watch a small war wage behind those green eyes of hers. I know Maisey, she's independent and doesn't ever want anyone's help, but I can also see she's weighing up her options.

She's a smart woman—very smart, in fact, so I know she's going to give in. Two is better than one, after all.

"Okay, fine. Two of us doing this is better than one," she grumbles, pointing to the string of lights at my feet. "So, maybe hand me those and then steady the ladder while I get the first hook sorted, okay?"

Am I smug? I am most certainly smug. Not only do I know what she's thinking, but I know the way she thinks. Which should be impressive, but it's also a little scary.

I grab the end of the lights Craig had been holding on to and hand them off to Maisey, before placing my foot on the bottom rung of the ladder to steady it. I can't help but watch Maisey from the vantage point I've been given below her, not only to make sure she won't fall, but it gives me a whole other angle where I can appreciate her body...and not in a creepy way.

Small town, same gym. I see her working out sometimes or jogging in the summer months when it's warmer. I'm not a monk, and I'd have to be dead to not notice her athletic figure, the way her hair blows in the wind when she's running, and the way her skin glistens and glows after she takes a yoga class.

"Hey, are you listening, Jack?"

Maisey's off the ladder and standing in front of me, her eyes narrowed and one hand placed solidly on her hip.

"Sorry." Busted. May as well own it. Now's not the time to let her know I'm over here appreciating the United States of Maisey. "I was daydreaming. What did you say?"

Cue rolling of the eyes. Yep, there it is. Jack McCoy, you get twenty bonus points. She points to the lights in my hand and gestures toward the ladder.

"I said, I'm moving the ladder this way, can you please move the lights the opposite way so I don't get tangled in them?" We both look at the giant tangle at our feet on the sidewalk around us. "Craig was in the middle of undoing this knotty mess. So it's my gift now."

"He did leave for a good cause," I remind her.

Maisey chuckles. "He left because he has a crush on the delivery driver. Did he look like he was upset that he, the head chef, had to go pick up our meat delivery?"

Thinking about it, she has a point. The Craig I know likes to hang out in the kitchen and that's about it. "Well, it's kismet I was here today, then."

Maisey drags the ladder over to the other side of the cafe's front bay window, stepping around the lights as best she can. "You work across the street, Jack."

"Actually, I came over here so I could talk to you." I trail behind her, moving lights as fast as I can, trying to keep them from tangling further and in general, attempting to be helpful. I feel like I'm failing when Maisey steps backward and her foot slips into the middle of a giant tangle. It's the kind of insane tangle that looks like it's had the last 365 days to get more knotted, and darn if it hasn't.

Gripping the ladder with both hands, Maisey gets one foot on the bottom rung while the other foot catches in the Christmas light bear trap she's trying to kick off. I hold my hands up to stop her.

"Stop moving, Maisey." Kneeling before her and grabbing the cluster, I gently pull strands apart, hoping to help break up the noose around her ankle. "Each movement and this thing seems to get tighter."

"You're telling me," she growls, kicking her foot out, after I told her not to, in a jerking fashion. While she probably thinks it'll help, neither one of us is prepared for what comes next.

Maisey kicks her foot out and it connects perfectly on the tip of my jaw. I suddenly understand when someone says they see the light when they're injured, because I sure do.

The side of my face feels like it's been slammed with a brick, and I look up in time to see one very beautiful woman tumbling from her perch, even if it is only from the first rung, thrown off-balance by the Christmas lights. There's no time for any thought or reaction because as she flails, Maisey reaches out and grabs at the first thing she can get a hold of to stabilize herself.

It's me. She grabs at me, but I'm not prepared. I'm in no way stable.

In the moments that follow, there are a few things I'll never forget. One of them is the sound of Christmas music piping out of the speakers lining Main Street, another is the look of shock etched on Maisey's face as she falls on top of me.

The last item? It would be the way my body felt as she slammed into my chest and sent us both crashing into a giant box labeled "Mistletoe."

CHAPTER 5

Maisey

The world around me spins, my neck hurts, and something resembling the feel of a hand is jammed into my abdomen. The faint smell of greenery assaults my senses while the sound of cars driving past fills my ears. Sitting upright, I rub the lump forming on the top of my head and open my eyes to find Jack staring at me intently.

"You okay?" He leans in close, so we're nose to nose. The exact perfect distance so I catch a whiff of *him*. Who would have thought Jack McCoy would smell like pine trees, fresh sheets, and lemons. Of course, I also detect a subtle smokey note as well. Hmm—smoked pine laundry detergent. I can see the tagline now: "Helping you put out the fires in your life one load of laundry at a time."

While the world around me is blurry, I'm one hundred percent aware of Jack's arms wrapped around my waist and the way he's holding me tightly against his chest. Only calling it simply a chest is quite possibly the rudest thing ever. This is a hard, sculpted chunk of man I'm leaning into, and he smells delicious. Something inside me flutters, but I slap it down, and real quick, too.

Traitorous fluttering. We don't flutter for Jack McCoy, remember?

Part of me feels like I could be concussed. I'm confused and lying here surrounded by who knows what. It feels like shrubbery is in my grasp, so I hold a clump up for inspection. Opening one eye, I can only describe my enthusiasm as royally pained. The foliage in my grasp makes it perfectly clear to see we've fallen in a box full of mistletoe.

Opening my other eye, there's a very concerned man peering at me, with a half-smile draped across those full lips of his.

Note to self: do NOT look at Jack's lips again, or risk being turned to mush.

"Hey." Jack's voice is but a whisper. He pushes a few strands of hair out of my face. "That was quite a fall. You okay?"

I'm lying in your arms, staring at your lips, and wondering if I need mouth-to-mouth, how do you think I'm doing?

Squeezing my eyes shut, I snap them open again before scrambling to my feet. Fast.

"I'm fine." I'm not fine, I'm mad—furious really. Mad at Craig for leaving, furious with Jack for being here, but also just irked I'm having to deal with any of this at all.

Jack springs up and stands beside me. "Look, Maisey, I came over here because I wanted to get a chance to say I'm sorry."

A chill crawls across my spine, and I have a knee-jerk reaction where I want to protect myself right away. Crossing my arms in front of my chest, I give Jack what I would describe as my best quizzical expression. "What, pray tell, are you sorry for? You didn't tangle the lights."

Jack clasps his hands in front of him, his mood a touch more somber than it was a moment ago. "I think you know why I'm apologizing, and it's not because of what just happened."

Of course I know why he's apologizing. I've been waiting months for this apology. I've daydreamed about this man coming to me and begging for my forgiveness.

Okay, I'm exaggerating. I really don't need anyone to beg and I haven't been waiting, like with baited breath, for months on end. Ever since he asked me out and said he'd call again—and didn't—I've not wanted anything more than an explanation.

And yes, it's really that simple. Seeing as I am a woman, I feel I can speak to the fact we're really rather simple creatures. We like to be independent, but also want to be taken care of and sometimes taking care of us simply comes down to communicating with us. Talking. Like what Jack's attempting to do with me now.

"I do know what you're talking about." Picking up one end of the string of lights, I start stuffing them back into a cardboard box. Simply for leaving me alone and in distress, Craig's punishment for taking off mid-project is that he gets to put up these stupid lights when he's back. "Thank you for saying it, but all the same I can't accept it."

"You're welcome. I wanted to come sooner and say it, I just...wait." Jack scratches his head, keeping his fingers in hair and twisting it. "You can't accept my apology?"

"I said what I said." The sound of jingle bells fills the air around us, and I hold back a burst of laughter as Jack's head spins.

"Are those sleigh bells? Where is that coming from?"

"It's my new ringtone." Laughing, I hold my phone in the air. Saved by the jingle bell. "Hello?"

"Is this Maisey Montgomery?"

Grateful for the reprieve, I turn my back to Jack. "It is."

"I'm Eileen Noelle, the head of public relations for the

Mistletoe Lodge. Is it possible to get a photo of you and your fiancé so we can share it on our social media channels ahead of your getaway weekend?"

I'm not sick to my stomach, you're sick to your stomach.

Glancing up, I turn around and my eyes lock with Jack's, and I swear it feels like he can read my mind. I turn my body away again and lower my voice.

"Hmmm, a photo? You know I'll need to wait until I get home and look around for one that would be appropriate." Am I buying time right now so I can think of a good fib to get me out of this? Oh, you bet I am. I'm also aware this is my chance to back out and let this woman know I'm not going to come. They can pick another winner, right?

It's the right thing to do. Why won't my mouth form the words?

Eileen coughs on her end of the phone. "I'm sure you've got something from an engagement session or a family event? Anything at all, really, would be good—just something of the two of you."

"My fiancé is a bit camera shy so I need to ask if he minds. He's funny like that." Insert my nervous, high-pitched, fake laugh here.

"Well, if you could send one over, we'd really appreciate it. And a bio, too? It needs to have basic info like how you met, when you're getting married, how he proposed, all that fun stuff. Oh, and I need to make sure to email you a copy of your itinerary and also a list of photo opportunities we'd like to use while you're here."

As Eileen chatters away, I'm pretty sure my face loses all its color because Jack's hand is suddenly bracing my elbow. "Do you need to sit down?"

Shaking my head no, I jerk my arm away and take two giant steps around Jack in an effort to give us more space. Something flies past me and drops to the ground as I shake my head. Realizing it's mistletoe, my hand flies to my hair, and I start combing my fingers through it only to find some stray branches have made my head their home.

It's a perfect storm of a day, really. I need to comprehend what this woman is saying to me and Jack's presence doesn't help me in keeping my composure right now. Never mind the bushes of mistletoe I'm pulling out of my hair.

This whole situation is nuts.

"An itinerary." Swallowing, I put one hand to my forehead, trying to hold back the migraine that's threatening to begin. "And photographs of us, too? I'm sorry, Eileen, but I wasn't aware all of this was part of winning."

"It is!" Eileen's bubbly. Wedding planner bubbly. It's got to be hard being this effervescent at all times, but that is something I'll never have to worry about. "Any content we collect will be used for our website and in their comms, so please be ready. That reminds me, I'll send you a suggested list of clothing, too. Colors that would be good for the shoot as well as items you'll want because of the outdoor activities you'll be doing."

My brain is still trying to process the call when Eileen disconnects because she has to "bounce"—do people still say that? Looking up from my call, I'm happy when I see Dylan waving as she jogs across the street to us.

"Hey, Jack, Dad is looking for you." She jerks a thumb over her shoulder. "The regional fire marshal stopped in and needs you to sign some paperwork, and he needs it done now."

"Yeah, okay." Shoving his hands in his pockets, Jack turns to me, not quite making eye contact. "I don't think our conversation is finished, Maisey, so I'll try again later. I just want you to know I meant what I said."

Jack jogs in the direction of the firehouse, leaving me to wonder if I'm crazy in thinking the look on his face was one of disappointment when he saw Dylan. I tuck it away to think about later because Dylan's in front of me dancing in place.

"You know, I had a brilliant idea." Her eyes sparkle, and she gives me this smile she usually reserves for her dad when she wants something. I can appreciate she's got a good idea, but I've got bigger issues right now named Eileen. I quickly fill her in, and I'm just as quickly sorry I did it.

"Maisey Montgomery the first!" Dylan likes to add on kinship identities to anyone and everyone when she's shocked by their actions, thus why I'm dubbed the first. "I take it you didn't tell them about the other essay after we spoke?"

"No, because I figured it would go away." Even as the words fall out of my mouth, I want to take them back.

"Well, it isn't."

Score to Dylan for pointing out the bloody obvious. I pull open the front door of the cafe, holding it open for Dylan to enter before me. She does, but as she walks past, she makes a giant show of holding her stomach and fake laughing. "And stop that."

"You need me right now." Dylan plops herself on the first stool she comes to at the counter, tapping it to get my attention. "I told you, I came over because I have an idea. It's perfect."

"I appreciate your help, but I did it to myself, Dylan. In fact, I'm going to call Eileen back right now, tell her what I did, and let them pick another winner." Sighing, I realize I can't fight the feeling in my gut any longer. No one needs this much drama when all they want is to walk around an old estate at Christmas. Even if I am *this* close to getting to walk in my mom's footsteps at the holidays that I can almost taste it.

Dylan cocks her head to one side. "But you haven't asked Jack."

For the second time in a few days, my hackles raise. This time, I hear the beginning of Darth Vader's theme song playing as snapshots of Jack's face pop to mind like a movie montage introducing us to the villain.

"Ask Jack to come with me for a romantic getaway and be my fake fiancé?" Dylan's crazier than I am. "No way."

Jack McCoy is a good-looking, charming guy. Is he likable? Even though I'm mad at him, yes, I can say he would be likable to most folks. Just not the ones he asks out and ditches, but I digress.

"Maisey, I looked at the schedule at the fire station and he's the only person who is off this weekend, who you know, and who you could ask to do it. Unless you can think of anyone else? You can always ask one of your cooks. What's Craig doing this weekend?"

"Working. Because I'm gone, remember?" I don't want to admit I already went down the roster for my back of house employees, front of house, too. There is no one on either list I feel comfortable enough to ask to go, not that asking Jack would be of any comfort to me.

Funny thing is, now that I've thought about Jack, I can only think about Jack. Like today when he held me, I'd not noticed the curve of his bicep before or the way he rakes his fingers through his hair when he's worried or thinking.

Oh man, did I just think about Jack raking his fingers through his hair?

"Earth to Maisey."

I snap my head to my left, where Dylan leans on the counter with an incredulous look washing across her features. "Sorry, I zoned out."

"If you can get him to go with you, you have a chance to save your butt. Before you can say anything else, hear me out; this whole fake essay thing could go viral on you, Maisey. Not a good viral like the posts Ari does for your food truck, The Sweet Spot, on social media, but bad viral as in 'Owner of Red Bird Cafe in Lake Lorelei is a Fraud' kind of headlines."

Dylan's prediction makes me shiver. "Ugh, that's horrible clickbait. Why would you say that?"

"Because it can happen, and if you're not going to call them and tell them about the other essay or pull out of the contrast, this might be your only option."

"I could be looked at as someone who defrauds people?" I'm sick. The kind of sickness I can only equate to the time I had the flu but thought it was a good idea to eat peanut butter and cucumber sandwiches all morning while watching the Price is Right. I was ill before the Showcase Showdown and spent the next two days in the bathroom. Took me years to eat peanut butter or cucumbers again.

"Look, I know you've been mad at him, but he's a good guy and I'm pretty sure you could convince him to go. You only want to get there, right? To go and follow in your mother's footsteps. There is nothing that says you need to arrive together or even deal with each other when you get there. Ask for a rollaway bed, and just have him show up for any fiancé-like things. Before you know it, you'll be on your way home and you can go back to being mad at him again."

At some point while Dylan is talking, my head begins bobbing up and down on its own. Even my most inner self is in agreement with her. This could be a solution, as much as it pains me to consider it.

"If it makes you feel better, write up a contract so you both clearly know what to do. It will make it cleaner and easier." One of the personality traits I love most about Dylan is that she's never one to back down. It shows in her work as a firefighter, and in the way she helps her father run his garage.

"I don't know, Dylan. It could be really weird for me to ask him." *But I really want to go.*

"Do this Mistletoe thing, act like you're in love, then part ways." Dylan glances down at her watch. "Crap, I gotta go. I told Reid I'd help him study for his tests this weekend."

Dylan throws a wave over her shoulder as she walks out the front door, striding down the street and out of sight. Looking across at the firehouse, something in my tummy dips and I wonder if she's right.

Can I put aside my irritation and my pride long enough to get what I really want for Christmas?

CHAPTER 6

Jack

"Y ou're going to give me five more crunches, then you get a break." Reid towers above me, sipping on a bottle of artesian water and checking himself out in the mirror. Is he one of those guys who's full of himself and always at the gym, overcompensating? Nope. He's the kind of friend who tries to provoke me by being ridiculously irritating, yet also entertaining, when we work out. He's also a personal trainer, so when he offers to give me some sessions as a favor, I'm not going to say no.

While I make it my mission to hit the gym at least three times a week, around the holidays all of us at the firehouse increase our workouts and their intensity. Thanks to members of the community, most of my firefighters are working off the calories gained from scarfing down the Christmas treats residents bring into the station.

I'm looking at you, third grade class of Lake Lorelei Elementary School...and those amazing gingerbread men you brought by earlier.

In between reps, while I fight cramps, Reid practices his

best Blue Steel modeling look in the mirror. Again. "Is it me or are you giving yourself more lingering looks that usual?"

"Ouch." Reid winces, physically reacting to my words. Nonplussed, he spins in a circle on his heel, facing the mirror full-on with his hands on his hips. Dragging his eyes up and down his body, he shoots me a side glance like he wants to make sure I'm witnessing this. He curls one arm, showing off a bicep. "There's a lot here to linger on. What's your point?"

Finishing my last rep, I hold my hand out, pointing in the direction of my water bottle.

"And you wonder why you're single." He hands me the bottle, and after taking a swig, I tip it in his direction. "A little more humbleness, you'd have the ladies eating out of your hand."

No sooner are the words out of my mouth when Maisey walks past us on her way to the treadmill. I don't think she sees me, at least there's no fire flashing in her eyes or sudden movement to leave. Seeing the AirPods in her ears, I can only assume she's lost in a playlist or listening to one of those true crime podcasts she likes so much.

How do I know this much about her? Back when we were actually friendly a few months ago, we were at a wedding exchanging recommendations of our favorite podcasts. I listened, okay? She'd just given me her top five when I asked her out, so yes, the memory is still burned into my brain, thank you very much.

Maisey's entrance doesn't go unnoticed by Reid, who cuts his eyes my way. "So, when are you going to write that book you mentioned? The one about how I can have the ladies eating out of my hand? Curious so I can make sure to buy a copy."

Grabbing the first thing I see, I sling the hand towel the gym gave me to wipe off the equipment in Reid's direction, striking gold when it bounces off his forehead.

"Roll out those legs and then we'll finish up with some stretching." Reid grabs a foam roller and positions it under my legs, winking as he helps me get in place. "Should leave you plenty of time to stop by and say hello to a certain cafe owner before you go to work."

"I have no idea what you mean." I hike myself up on my hands, moving my body back and forth on the roller, massaging my muscles and working out the last of the knots.

"Dude. Jack." Reid shakes his head as he kneels beside me and lowers his voice. "I've known Maisey for a long time; she's friends with my sister. Since they work together, I've really gotten to know her even more the last year."

It doesn't escape me that I'm being given love-life advice in the middle of a packed gym first thing in the morning, and the advice is coming from Reid Shannon. Do I trust Reid? I mean, sure, when it comes to saving my butt in the middle of a fire or having my back when a building is about to light up. But for advice like this? The jury's still out.

Searching the mirror, I quickly spy Maisey on the other side of the gym falling into a rhythm on her treadmill. Her hair is pulled up on top of her head in that messy bun she does, where a few strands are left hanging loose to frame her face. The sun shines through the window, giving her an almost ethereal look from where I'm sitting. I can even see beads of perspiration starting on the back of her neck. My eyes can't help but follow said trail and its glistening pattern as it threads its way down her back and through her shoulder blades, disappearing where her tank top dips about midway down her back.

"What would your sister say to do, then?" Fine, if he's going to give me advice, I'm going to lean into it. I'd ask what could go wrong, but I feel like I'm inviting Murphy and that terrible law of his to dinner if I do.

"Ari would tell you to keep at it, don't give up." Reid pulls the blue foam roller out from under me, placing it back by the wall for the next user. "Why are you so intent on making up with Maisey now, anyway? You stood her up."

"I didn't stand her up!" The joy of living in a small town. Everyone knows your business and they know their version of the truth, which is usually close to but still a far cry from what actually transpired. Like in this case.

"Well." Reid inclines his head in Maisey's direction. "Tell her that."

Reid's frighteningly correct. While I want to make up with her—and I really do—I also need her now for this weekend. She's my reason to get out of Lake Lorelei before Cupid's helpers arrive.

Reid looks at his watch and claps my shoulder. "Gotta go to my next appointment, but I'll see you next week."

I wait until Reid's gone before I make a move and leave the safety of my workout space. Keeping my eyes trained on Maisey, I walk over to where she's jogging away, probably running from whatever criminal or serial killer story she's listening to. Scratch that, Maisey's the kind of woman who would run toward them to fight them off. She's scrappy—another one of the many things I like about her.

Luckily, the treadmill beside her is empty. As discreetly as I can, I hop on and start the machine, even making sure the safety key that turns it off is hooked into place. Nerdy? Yes, but I'm a safety nerd. I set my treadmill for a gentle walk and wait, like a snake in the grass, for her to look my way.

There's a blissful few moments where I can tell she has no idea I'm here. We jog side by side, matching breath for breath, and I feel like we're perfectly in sync. Some part of me is wondering if this could be a sign; maybe just maybe she'll look over and be happy to see me—but she's so tuned into her own world, she's not noticed me yet.

I keep running, inching up the speed a few clicks at a time

until I'm trotting at a quick pace, but not wanting to go too fast. We'd done a leg workout this morning, so my legs are nothing but jelly now. The more I walk, the more exhausted I feel, and the realization hits that it wasn't a smart idea to hop on here after such a big workout.

Glancing down at the computer screen, I decide to give myself two more minutes, then I'll hop off if Masiey hasn't noticed me. Even if she has, and she's chosen to ignore me, that's fine, too. I'm starting to get the hint. My eyes drift out the window and across the parking lot, and I'm moving on to my to-do list that's waiting for me when I get to work when the belt screeches to a sudden halt. Everything suddenly stops. Except me.

There's a moment of confusion, but I'm told later that my forward roll off the treadmill will forever be seen as *the* Olympic gymnastics move to beat in years to come. It was part cartwheel, part me losing my balance and not having stable footing, and part jogging with nowhere to go except over the top of the treadmill and onto the floor on the other side.

It was one hundred percent embarrassing.

"Jack!" Maisey kneels beside me, shaking my shoulder gently. "Oh, wow. I am so sorry. I didn't think that would happen."

Opening my eyes, I find two bright green ones flashing in front of me. Her eyes are usually more emerald green, but the sun brings out a sliver of blue I haven't noticed before. Probably because we've not been this close since the night I asked her out. I can taste her breath, if that's a thing.

"I'm okay, I think." Maisey helps me sit up, and I'm aware of a few other members of the gym now crowding around us. When the manager comes over, I let him know I'm fine and promise to come by his office if I start feeling like my injury is worse.

Once everyone disperses, leaving Maisey and I alone, I set this woman in my sights.

"What did you mean when you said you didn't think that would happen?"

Biting her bottom lip, she holds up the safety key. A quick look at my treadmill verifies what I know to be true.

Maisey pulled my safety key out while I was running on the treadmill.

"To be fair, when I grabbed it you were only jogging at the same speed of a fast walk." She holds out the key, placing it in the palm of my hand with her eyes downcast. "I don't know why I did it, Jack. I'm really sorry."

"You're sorry?"

"Very. I've just been really crazy lately. There's a lot going on. But you didn't deserve that...whatever that was."

Leaning against the wall, I tilt my head off to one side and grin. "Thank you. I accept your apology."

Masiey's face is incredulous. "You do?"

I shrug. "Yep. I do. You made a mistake, so I forgive you."

"I know what reverse psychology is, Jack." Huffing, Maisey plops down on the ground next to me, leaning against the wall as well. "I just sent you falling—no, not falling —*flying* over your treadmill like a ten-year-old kid going over the handlebars of their bike and you can forgive me"—she holds up a hand in the air and snaps her fingers—"like that?"

"I can. It's how I was raised."

If I was a betting man, I'd put twenty dollars down that if there was a white flag around, Maisey would be waving it right now. We sit in silence for a minute or two longer before she sighs and crosses her legs, turning her body so we face one another.

"And so was I."

"I was counting on that, because I need you to tell me how

I can fix things with you, Maisey. I mean it. What can I do to make it up to you?"

She sighs again and closes her eyes. "You know, I can't believe I'm asking you, but there is something you can do. But you're probably busy this weekend like everyone else in this town."

"Actually, if we're being honest...."

"...and we are," she acknowledges.

"Well, I'm trying to avoid my mother this weekend." I lean in closer to Maisey so I can keep my voice low, but catch a whiff of her shampoo. Watermelon? So good. "My mother and grandmother are trying to set me up on some blind dates, and according to my sources, it's in the guise of a family get-together this Saturday. Anything I can do to not be around, I'll do."

"Before we launch into the topic of blind dates—plural? —I want to clarify." Maisey's eyebrows arch. "Anything?"

"I overheard Dylan talking to Reid and Dub at work, and I know you need someone to go with you to the Mistletoe Lodge this weekend." Placing my hand on my heart, I look her in the eyes. "I am happy to be your fake fiancé; I just need you to get me away from this whole matchmaking scenario I'm about to be thrust into."

"You would go with me, away from the safety of your own home, even after the way I've acted and treated you?"

"It's not about you anymore, it's about me now, too. The way I see it, you need me as much as I need you and we can be of use to each other." Watching her face, I can see she's amenable to the suggestion, but I'm still not sure if she's signed on for the whole thing. "We can go separately to the Mistletoe, if you want, so you don't have to be in a car with me. If that makes it easier."

"Please, Jack, I'm not that much of a grump. We can ride in the same car." Maisey laughs as she grips the base of the treadmill and uses it to help her stand up. "But we'll split the bill for the gas. Inflation, you know."

"Fine. Anything else?"

Maisey holds up a finger before she walks over to the front desk. The receptionist hands her a pen and a sheet of paper, and then Maisey's on her way back to me. Parking herself on the ground beside me again, she puts pen to paper and scribbles away madly.

"To keep things clear between us, we're going to have a contract." She tucks a stray hair behind an ear and taps her cheek with the pen. When I lean in to see if I can make out what she's writing, I get a heady rush from a subtle hint of hyacinths and lilacs mixed with that watermelon fragrance again. I fight the creepy urge to lean in and take a quick sniff of Maisey, and luckily she shoves the paper in front me at the same time, stopping me from any awkward explanation of why my nose is buried in her hair.

"Here, I've outlined a loose agreement for us." She points to the bullet points she made. "This is a layout of what our relationship can look like."

"'This contract includes but is not limited to...' Do you even know what this verbiage means, Maisey?"

"No clue, but go on. Keep reading. You'll get the jist."

"Okay. 'This contract includes but is not limited to: hand-holding, hugs, and general doting couple activities to give off the impression we are in love and engaged.'"

"Strategically timed hand-holding and close hugs when others are around. It will make people think we're a loving couple, right?"

I hold up the paper in my hands. "According to this we will be."

Maisey bobs her head up and down. "Indeed."

Glancing back at the contract in my grasp, I find item two on the list. "TBD kisses."

"TBD." Maisey's skin flushes. "It's TBD because we need to discuss this part. Since we're engaged, the publicist and her team expect some kind of affectionate display, so I figure we'll want to do at least one kiss for a photo there. We'll need to be prepared for that."

"Publicist?" She's going into marketing speak and I'm still wrapping my head around the fact we're scheduling a kiss. Lest we forget that just under an hour ago this woman didn't want me anywhere near her.

"There are some things we need to do once we're there, but that will be in our itinerary. It's not anything for you to worry about right now."

I put my hands in the air like she's got me backed into a corner because let's face it: she kind of does. I want to make things right—and I need to get out of town. It just so happens Maisey is the only one who can save me and in the best way possible.

I mean, who would say no to this adventure?

"You know, I think I may need an addendum added if they're going to have us doing couple-things at the Mistletoe."

"You get to stay at a luxury resort for two nights. Free." Maisey rolls her eyes. "And remember, we're engaged so the stakes are going to be a little higher."

"How much higher?"

"I was told there are some events at the estate that they'll want us to be a part of so they can take some photos of us, as the winners, having fun. I'm thinking it's a sleigh ride, probably shopping in the Christmas village, maybe we pet a reindeer... I doubt it's anything major. But, we'll need to be—"

I see where this is going.

" —a couple very much in love."

"You got it."

Maisey signs on the dotted line before handing me the pen

so I can do the same. "Now, I need to take a photo of the two of us to send them. They want it for their social media."

Pointing to my sweat-soaked shirt, I tilt my head to the side. "Sure you want to do it now?"

She thinks for a moment before responding. "You're right. We should both be cleaned up for it, so I'll come by the station on my way home and we'll take one then?"

"Alright." I stand up first, turning around and putting my hand out to help Maisey. Only she's already on her feet and ready to go.

Maisey thrusts her hand out and grabs mine, pumping it up and down. "Looks like we have a deal. But, I reserve the right for things to go back to how they were once we return home. Got it?"

Like she'll want that when I'm done. Maisey has agreed to give me a second chance, whether she likes it or not, and I'm going to take full advantage of my opportunity.

I've always had the utmost respect for Maisey—who doesn't in this town? She's a savvy businessperson, she loves her community and stands up for it all the time at town meetings, and yes, she's also a beautiful woman. Inside and out.

To be honest, she intimidates me. She seems to have it all together, everyone in this town loves her and backs her while I'm a bit of a flag waving loosely without a tether on the flagpole. Swaying back and forth, flippity-floppity in the wind, always unsure about settling down with anyone, never mind dating for any extended period of time. The one time I took a chance with anyone since moving here and put myself out there, I was reeled back in when personal tragedy struck, rocking my plans.

But she doesn't know any of this, she only knows I didn't show up. And right now Maisey is standing in front of me shaking my hand. To me, it's as good as it gets when it comes to touching this woman.

I'll take it. "Maisey, you have got a deal."

"Fabulous." Tucking the contract under her arm, she walks away, calling out over her shoulder as she does, "I'll forward you the email the PR team sent me and will be by your office in a few hours."

I wait until Maisey's car has pulled out of the parking lot before I head into the locker room to change. There's a quick pit stop at my locker so I can text Etta the news I won't be around this weekend, and when I hit send, my heart all but leaps out of my chest.

I'm a fan of second chances—and now I get this weekend to get back into Maisey's good graces. To explain what happened and see if she'll give me another chance, too.

Fingers crossed.

The drive from Lake Lorelei to the Mistletoe Lodge usually takes about an hour, but today with Jack at the wheel, and because it's a Friday, it feels like it's taken us a lot longer. Normally, I'm the type to insist someone pulls over and lets me drive—I claim anxiety, but in reality it's because I like to go as fast as possible. I've been told I have a lead foot.

However, since I've agreed to a temporary truce with Jack for the purpose of this weekend, I'm going to attempt to sit back and roll with things. Even when Jack insists we stop for hot chocolates at a roadside Christmas tree stand because we "have to," I don't try to stop him. This man is going out of his way to do me a solid and I can't spit at it.

"We're not far now." Taking the last swig of my salted caramel hot chocolate, I finally looked up from my mobile phone long enough to realize how close we are to the lodge. I've been replying to emails and pretty much acting like I'm really busy on my side of the car so I don't have to make small talk. We agreed to a truce, which I think essentially means I've agreed not to be so snarky. We don't have to braid each other's hair.

Jack sings along to Billy Joel, and his voice is surprisingly good. He turns the volume down on the radio before pointing to a sign on the side of the road. "It's two exits away."

"Are you sure you're ready for this?" My stomach kicks up a fuss, like a couple of angry raccoons are having a fist fight inside me. I flick open my email, opening the one from Eileen with the subject line ROMANTIC WEEKEND GETAWAY CHECK IN. "Look, I can understand if you just want to do your own thing when we get there, Jack. I don't expect you to hang out with me the whole time. We'll look at the itinerary and can put on a show when we have to. I know this whole thing has got to be feeling weird to you because I know it feels super weird to me."

Mr. Easy Breezy shrugs. "I'm in it for whatever, Maisey. We're engaged, remember? Happy wife, happy life."

"But we're not really engaged, so you don't need to be in character now." Glancing at the phone in my hands, I realize we've forgotten one tiny detail. Holding up my left hand, I point to my ring finger. "We're already failing as a newly engaged couple. We don't even have a ring yet."

"No problem." Jack taps the wheel and purses his lips together, activating his thinking face. How do I know that's what it is? Because it's the same one he uses when he needs to decide if he's going to have the Monday lunch special or his usual steak sandwich on toasted rye, hold the mayo, add a side of mustard. "How about we tell them when we got engaged it was spur of the moment, so we decided to deal with the ring later—and now we haven't had time to pick one out yet."

"Ohhh, that's good. We'll go with that." I look down at my hands and rub them together, massaging my fingers one by one nervously. For some reason this small act has always calmed me down, and I'm sure it goes without saying I'm now in need of a full-on hand massage. I'm so wired. There's a mixture of ridiculous excitement brewing inside me about finally getting to go to the Mistletoe Lodge, but it's sprinkled with apprehension and worry.

Jack hits the turn signal as he maneuvers the car off the highway onto our exit ramp. A giant green sign tells me we're less than five miles away from the estate. My heart blows up, while the raccoons keep scraping with one another in my tummy.

Deep breaths, Maisey. It's all going to be fine.

Jack slows down, bringing the car to a stop at a traffic light at the end of the exit. Out of the corner of my eye, I see he's watching me.

"You know, you never did tell me why you want to come here so badly," he says.

"It's the tour of the private art gallery that really interests me." With all of the nonchalance I can muster, I lift one shoulder and let it drop, before pulling my hair off my shoulder and wrapping it in a low bun at the base of my neck. I really don't want, nor do I need, Jack knowing my reasons for being here. "I've wanted to do the special Christmas tour for a few years now, but with the cafe I've been too busy. But a private tour is included in the winner's package—according to the research I did online, they open up parts of the art gallery they normally don't when they host the private tours."

"I've read that, too. I also know they're opening up the Madison and Johnson room for the holiday and putting out their special collection of snow globes for viewing this year."

My jaw goes slack and my head snaps to attention as soon as Jack lets that little fact roll off his tongue. Am I sitting beside a fellow Mistletonian?

I turn sideways in my seat so I'm facing him. "How do you know about the snow globes?"

"I have women in my family who are infatuated with those

globes." Jack screws up his face, rolling his eyes and poking his tongue out of his mouth like he's gagging. Luckily he's on my left side so I can swat him, but only so hard. "I'm joking, but I did grow up around one snow globe fanatic in particular. My grandmother. She's been collecting them since the Mistletoe Lodge started the tradition of putting out branded globes at Christmas way back in the 1940s. Let's just say the genes were passed down and now the women in my family love helping her collect the snow globes, too."

Wow. If we were scoring our path to peace, I'd say Jack has just logged twenty points for his team. I'm impressed, but still it *is* Jack and therefore I'm still wary. Cute story or not, I'm on a mission and he's got an appearance to keep up.

Turning my attention back to our check-in email, I scan my eyes over it to see if there's any other info we need to know. "I don't see it listed in the email Eileen sent, but I'm pretty sure we'll get to view the snow globes privately. I'm also going to make sure to ask for a rollaway bed once we're checked in. I figure the more discreet I can be, the better, so I'll do it after hours because we're 'waiting until we get married' before we share a bed."

"You're good." Jack shakes his head and laughs. "You've got it all figured out, haven't you?"

"I hope so." I hold up two hands with crossed fingers on each.

Ahead of us on the side of the road is a giant antique-looking wooden sign pointing us down a long and winding tree-lined drive. The entrance to the Mistletoe Lodge. Slowing down, Jack puts on his blinker to signal his turn while simultaneously I take a breath and inhale so deeply, I start coughing.

Something taps my arm and Jack hands me a bottle of water. "Here, drink this and take a few deep breaths. Get your nervousness out now, because once we go over that rise up ahead, we're in this thing for the weekend. Together."

I take a sip of the water before sitting up taller in my seat. He's right. It's just a few days, and nothing will go wrong if I stick to the script. Handing the bottle back to him, I sweep my arm out in front of me. "Let's do this."

Giant pine trees speckled with faux snow line the driveway on both sides, creating a winter wonderland feel as we drive into the estate. In the spirit of the holiday season, the staff at the estate have gone to the trouble of threading Christmas lights through all of the trees, and have planted what looks like handmade wooden candy canes about three feet tall on either side of the road, giving off the feeling of a hidden Christmas village just beyond.

As we drive over the hill and crest the top, my breath hitches when I see the estate in front of us. The Mistletoe Lodge sits on one edge of the property, while the tiny village they added in later years sits on the other, creating its own little community tucked away in the mountains.

More faux snow dots the hillside, most likely man-made that morning and styled for the day to welcome visitors as they arrive for their holiday getaways, last minute shopping, or to simply enjoy the ambiance of North Carolina's only North Pole Village which sits on the property of the lodge, also known as the Merriest Place on Earth. And if it's not the merriest on Earth, it's at least the merriest in all of North Carolina, that's for sure.

Holiday music plays around us, "White Christmas" mysteriously filling the air—and I say mysteriously because I can't see where the speakers are hidden. It's like we're entering an adult version of Disneyland—if you're into Christmas on steroids and minus the mice.

Coming closer to the tiny village, we follow the signs leading us to the circular driveway in front of the main entrance of the Mistletoe Lodge itself.

As we drive through the gates and see what lies before us,

those raccoons, the ones who had stopped fighting in my stomach, decide it's time to do more damage. One of them breaks out, goes rogue, and sets off a tiny explosion instead.

Outside the main entrance are several staff members, all lined up and standing at attention, and all of them dressed in their finest and crispest uniforms. Garland drapes everywhere the eye can see, and a pair of giant Christmas trees have been placed in planters beside the concierge desk, twinkling away.

"Wow." Jack lets out a low whistle beside me. "They must have someone famous coming in. Or royalty. They don't have to do this every day, do they?"

"No idea, but I'm getting some serious Downton Abbey vibes like nobody's business." Shivering, I grab my purse and pull on my coat, shoving my arms inside and wrapping it around my body. "If you pull up on the other side of the concierge, I'll go check us in."

Jack brings the car to a stop. Gripping the door handle, I lean my weight against it ready to hop out—and the world around me shifts.

There's a blur of fabric and concrete, and a rush of activity around me. A blast of cold hits my skin and slaps my cheeks. When I'm able to focus my vision again, I'm flat on my back and on the ground, with at least a dozen staff members looming above me, trying to help me up.

Judging by the amount of people lined up in front of me, and the flair which surrounds everything, one would think we've arrived at Buckingham Palace. It appears that everyone who works here, and probably ever has, is lined up to greet us —from the concierge to the front desk staff, housekeepers, and even members of the kitchen staff.

"I'm so sorry, I went to open the door at the same time you got out." One of them, wearing a name tag that says Clark, looks at me with concern. "That was quite a tumble. My sincerest apologies."

"I'm fine and it's so nice to meet you." I shake Clark's hand and brush myself off, hoping I can brush off the last sixty seconds as well. Jack is at my side as well, chewing back his laughter.

"We're all very excited to have you both here." Clark turns to Jack, shaking his hand, too. "You and your beautiful fianceé."

"Thank you." Jack says as he wraps an arm around my shoulders. My first instinct is to shrug it off, but as I do Jack grips my arm and pulls me in tighter. A gentle reminder we're faking it, but we're in love as of now. "This is our first getaway since we've been engaged. Just me and the missus."

The very pointy part of my elbow finds its way to the perfect location between two of Jack's ribs when I nudge him. Is there a creepy smile on my face like I'm a contestant in a Miss Mistletoe pageant? You bet there is. I should have put Vaseline on my teeth to keep my lips moist.

"So sweet! Someone, snap a photo, please." A slim brunette steps forward, grabbing my hand and pumping it up and down twice as a flash goes off, blinding me. "I'm Eileen. It's nice to finally meet you. Welcome and congratulations."

"Thank you, Eileen. It's nice to be here." I pull my hand away, ready to continue to the front desk, but Eileen has other plans. She makes this clear when she shoves a folder in my hands and turns her head to address Jack, whose arm is still snug around my shoulders.

I hold the folder up in the air. "What's this?"

"Just a few items we need to have you tick off while you're here, all part of your itinerary. There are some expectations we have for the two of you as part of the prize package, but our goal is to let you two have a peaceful and romantic getaway. Especially after all you've been through with the loss of Stuart."

"Oh, well, you know." My stomach feels like one of Lake

Lorelei's fire trucks has just driven through it. I don't even remember writing this white lie down, but obviously I did. I've stooped to a new low. I wanted to win this so badly I used my cat who died earlier in the year as ammunition.

Unsure how to react to her statement, I thread my fingers through Jack's free hand and snuggle in close to his body, that fresh sheet scent hitting my nose. "This is why I wanted to make sure this guy got a few days away to clear his head. He was very close to Stuart, and Jack loves Christmas so much, I thought this was a great gift for him."

"I do love Christmas," Jack says, nodding beside me. "I really do."

"That's what Maisey's entry said, actually." Eileen is starting to scare me. Let's face it, I can't blame it on her, but I wish I could remember everything I wrote down now.

"It did?" Jack's hand grips mine a little tighter. "She's been tight-lipped about her entry. Can you tell me what my sweet gal wrote?"

Eileen grins, her eyes hopping back and forth from Jack's to mine. "She said you were a sucker for sleigh rides, you love hot chocolate piled with whipped cream, and may have mentioned you grew up working for your family's farm."

"My family's...farm?" Jack croaks beside me. I shove my body into his, cuddling my faux-fiancé. Add a touch of batting my eyelashes and attempting to look cute, and you've got me. Right here, groveling as quietly as I can. My eyes meet Jack's and using no words, I'm literally begging him with my eyes to play along.

"You know, hon-ey...the farm. The one you told me all the stories about." Slapping his arm playfully, I extricate myself and lean toward Eileen. "He's quite reserved, this one. Not one to talk about himself nor one to amplify his awesomeness, if you know what I mean."

"Yes," Jack growls as he removes his arm from my shoulder

and slips it around my waist, pressing his lips to the top of my head. "I'm very low-key about how amazing I am, but this one time I'll let you brag about me."

"Oh goodness, you two are so cute." Eileen holds up her phone and snaps a photo, taking time to look at her work approvingly after. "We'll post that in a story on Instagram later. So good."

When I see her bury her nose in her phone, I clear my throat to get her attention. "Eileen, I know we just arrived, but I'm curious when we'll get the private tour of the art gallery I read about as part of the prize?"

"Oh yeah," Jack pipes in, "and the snow globes."

"Fans, are we?" Eileen's eyebrows arch in surprise. "We can discuss that later; right now I want to get you two settled in." Her head spins left to right as she scans the small crowd. "Where's Theo?"

A thin man in a butler's uniform steps forward, bowing at the waist. "Here, ma'am."

"Fabulous." Eileen turns to us. "Theo is your personal butler for the weekend. He's here to help you with anything you need. Theo, will you take care of their bags and take them to their suite?"

"Yes, ma'am." Theo turns to us, his kind smile already warming my heart as he holds out his hand to shake mine. "And hello, Maisey. What time are we to have Santa's Sleigh ready for the two of you to go out this afternoon?"

I can't help the laughter that spills out. "I'm sorry, but did you really mean it when you said we had a sleigh?"

"You most certainly do." Eileen gestures down the driveway where a giant red sleigh with one horse attached sits next to a sign that says "Sleigh Parking Only." She then opens a folder identical to the one she gave me and points to something inside. "You'll be taking the sleigh into our Christmas village to do some shopping and sightseeing. So, Theo, please have the sleigh ready by 3 PM."

In a flurry, everyone disperses as we march behind Theo, who carries our bags, and Eileen, who leads us into an elevator which whisks us up a few floors. Within fifteen minutes of our arrival on the estate grounds, we're already in the safety of our suite.

Turning a key in the lock of the main door, Eileen turns triumphantly to the two of us. "Welcome to your master suite."

To call this room luxurious would be an understatement. It's a one-bedroom layout, and while it's been styled impeccably to suit the holiday season, I can only focus on the sofa across the room. Fighting the urge to pump my fist, a wave of relief washes over me. I hope it's comfy because that's where Jack's going to be sleeping for the next two nights. After seeing all of this effort they've gone to, and sensing the expectation that's on us, there is no way we can ask for a rollaway bed now.

"So," Eileen begins, clearing her throat, "since I never got a bio from you, Maisey, I wanted to ask when is the big day? It's part of the story we're telling about the two of you for our marketing campaign. We want to mention how you came here to relax ahead of your wedding day. The powers that be on our executive floor want to see it's a real couple we have in house. It will make them happy."

I feel the blood drain from my face. "Why's that?"

"The board wanted us to add fine print in the rules saying the winners must be engaged to enter. Otherwise we reserve the right to bill you for the stay and for all the prizes, and we won't be able to use any of the photos or content we create with you for our upcoming campaigns. Which would be a horrific outcome for all of us. I'd lose my job..." She trails off for a second before laughing. "Obviously, the two of you are the real deal. And we're glad that we can make your dream come true and gift you a romantic getaway."

Am I sick? Do I feel bad? Yes to both, but a quick glance at my purse reminds me I'm also here for my own reasons.

"Obviously." It's the only response I can come up with.

"So." Eileen's eyes bounce back and forth from Jack's to mine. "When is it?"

I have no clue what to say, so I simply start talking. "Well, we're still––"

"––trying to decide if we'll stay local or do a destination wedding." Jack's voice sweeps in like a warm hug wrapping itself around my body.

"Exactly." Looping my arm through Jack's, I smile at Eileen who watches us with narrowed eyes, as if we're under a microscope. "We're taking time now to enjoy being engaged, you know? Before the planning has to begin."

There's a moment of silence before a subtle smile begins making its way across her features. Visibly relaxing, she grins at both of us. "I can't blame you. There's so much to do and so much to plan, isn't there?" Eileen taps the folder in her hand. "Before I go, let's look at the itinerary we've planned for your stay."

Opening the folder, she points to a document in front of her and angles it so we can read what it says.

FRIDAY

2 PM: Early check-in and champagne reception
3 PM: Sleigh ride through Santa's village
5 PM: Hotel for interview for Mistletoe social media

SATURDAY

11:30 AM: Art gallery + snow globe tour (not open to public)
2PM: Couples massage
5 PM: Christmas tree lighting in hotel lobby

SUNDAY
11 AM: CHECK OUT

"It's pretty self-explanatory. Maybe, since Jack loves horses, we can sneak in a trail ride," Eileen murmurs as she turns down the volume of a lively walkie-talkie sitting on her hip. She points to an ice bucket complete with a champagne bottle and a canape spread laid out on a table across the room. "Please, take some time now to relax, enjoy some downtime, and sip on some bubbles while you try some of our chef's best hors d'oeuvres. All compliments of the Mistletoe."

That table may look incredible, but I'm fighting to keep my roadside snack of Grandma Utz's potato chips down. I knew I shouldn't have eaten the whole bag on the drive over and washed it down with that salted caramel hot chocolate. "Thank you."

"You're welcome. If you have any questions, you can let me or Theo know. We'll leave you two for now to get settled in."

Like an alarm clock, the walkie-talkie in her hand suddenly lights up, an orange button flashing as it crackles to life and pages for Eileen to report to reception.

With a curt nod from Eileen and a sweet bow from Theo, the pair hurry from our room, on to the next item up for business, leaving us all alone. No sooner does the door close when Jack spins on his heel and puts his hands on hips, the look on his face a touch stormier than I remember it being when we arrived.

He taps his foot, refusing to make eye contact with me. When he does finally look at me, I can feel his displeasure. It's like wearing a new wool sweater. It's rough and uncomfortable.

He crosses his arms. "Maisey, what have you gotten us into?"

CHAPTER 8

Jack

Saying yes to being someone's fake fiancé is one thing, but when small details begin popping up, ones you weren't warned about in advance, it can all be a bit… surprising. By the time Hurricane Eileen cleared out, we had just enough time to change before we had to meet the sleigh driver. So, Maisey and I still have some talking to do about surprises and getting our story straight.

"I knew we were engaged, but no one told me I was a sucker for sleigh rides, too." Turning toward Maisey, tucked under a blanket in the back of the sleigh, I expect to find her rolling her eyes at me as usual, but instead she's busy snapping photos of the countryside. Good way to avoid talking, but we're truly stuck together so it's not like she can avoid me the whole time. My inner voice tells me to relax; however, thinking back on the last few months, she actually could avoid me and has proven it to be true.

Pointing to the hot drink in my hands, she gives me her smuggest of the smuggy smiles. "So telling them you love a good artisan hot chocolate wasn't a nice thing to do?"

Do I like hot chocolate with piles of whipped cream? I do

and she's right, I'm grateful because Theo made sure I had one in my hands before we left the hotel.

"Yes, but not the point." I nudge her in her ribs with my elbow. "What possessed you to tell them I was born on a farm?"

Tilting my head I try, again, to get Maisey to look at me, but she won't make eye contact. Instead she turns back to the scenery, and I can't blame her. It's stunning—we're literally dashing through the snow, in a one-horse open sleigh. At this very moment. There's man-made snow as far as the eye can see, along with the weighted silence which only a blanket of snow brings, even if it is fake. It's downright magical.

"I did not say you were born on a farm, I said your family owned one." The quiet between us broken, Maisey's tone sounds like it's bordering on exasperated. She's playing it cool, but as soon as I see her start running her fingers through her hair and twisting strands around her little digits, I know. She's freaking out, like I am, about this whole thing. It makes perfect sense as to why Dylan didn't want to even deal with this headache, but there's part of me that thinks it's cute. "And it's not a farm; I told them you had a ranch. I had binge-watched Yellowstone so I had a one-track mind."

"Those are details which I should have known." Flipping through Eileen's folder, I pull out the itinerary and put it on my lap, pointing to the items I want her to pay attention to. "Sleigh ride. Tick. Interviews at the hotel before dinner? No problem. Touring the art gallery and snow globe exhibition... amazing! But 'sneaking in a trail ride' is not in my wheelhouse."

Still no eye contact, but there's a soft pink flush creeping to her cheeks and it's not from the wind. "You're a fireman, right?"

"Right," I say, nodding. "Not a rancher."

"But you're strong and you did tell me once you've ridden

a horse before." She turns to face me. "Plus, I've seen your workouts when it's arm day at the gym. If the ride happens, which it probably won't, you'll be fine."

If this is buttering me up, then that was well played by Miss Montgomery. "Is there anything else I need to know about our relationship or my life before we go any further?"

A wicked smile plays on Maisey's lips. Maisey's full, soft lips. I hadn't noticed until now that the pink in her cheeks almost perfectly matches the pink in her lips. Like cotton candy at the county fair.

Worried I've lingered in admiration a moment too long, my eyes flick to Maisey's. She watches me, and a shiver races across my skin as her eyes widen and she licks her lips, her hand flying to her mouth. "Are my lips chapped?"

Busted. But I can't let her know that I was ogling her lips and thinking about kissing them for the next five hours or the unforeseeable future. Reaching into my pocket, I pull out a tube of lip balm for the save. "They look like they could be. Here."

Plucking it from my hand, she pulls the cap off and places the balm to her lips, gliding it across her skin for coverage. I'm lost in thought and wishing I was that tube of lip balm when she snaps the cap back on and tosses it back to me.

"Thanks." Looking ahead, Maisey suddenly jumps and squeals with true delight as she pats my thigh. "Jack, look! We're here."

Our sleigh comes over a crest, and lo and behold, in front of us a scene I can only describe as Christmas to infinity. A sea of twinkling lights and pine trees greets us, one side of the village boasting a tiny home, which I assume based on the number of children threaded in a line around it, would be Santa's house. The town is not that big at all and it appears everything centers around one street. It's made to look like

Main Street USA, but it's full of nothing but Christmas-themed stores and restaurants.

Our driver expertly maneuvers the sleigh onto the streets of the happy village, pulling up in front of one of the quaint little stores. I hadn't noticed on the way over how similar he looks to Santa Claus, but when he turns around it's hard not to see the resemblance.

"I'll stay right here," his voice booms as his twinkling eyes flick from mine to Maisey's. "You two come back to get me when you're ready."

Hopping down from the sleigh, my feet hit the sidewalk and I nearly slip on a patch of black ice. Snow crunches underneath the soles of my shoes, yet nowhere close by has had any snow this year. I even looked it up on Google. This place has thought of everything.

I hand the blanket I had wrapped around me for the ride back to the driver. "So, does someone make snow every night to keep the whole winter wonderland vibe going?"

"It's all part of the Mistletoe experience." Our driver grins, bobbing his head up and down. "Every detail is orchestrated, down to the snowfall."

"That's so cool!" I hold my hand out to Maisey, who's attempting to climb out of the sleigh. "Did you know about the snow?"

She shakes her head, her face twisting into a grimace as she tries to get out. She points to one of her legs. "For some weird reason, I can't get my leg out. My pants are caught on something attached to the driver's seat and I can't quite reach it."

"Here." Propping my body against hers, I angle my shoulder at her hip to help lift her up and hopefully release her pants so she can get her leg out swiftly and easily. As soon as I wrap my arms around her upper thighs, she screams in my ear and sits back down in the seat.

My eyes all but cross, but the ringing eventually stops. "What was that about?"

Maisey wags a finger in my direction. "I don't need you to help me take my pants *off*, Jack."

"I'm not." Stepping forward, I indicate for her to stand up again. "I'm going to give you a boost so we can get your leg out. Just hold on to me when I pick you up. Got it?"

Maisey looks at me like I've suggested we ask Prince Harry to come hang out for dinner tonight and after, maybe Meghan Markle will give her a pedicure. "I don't know, Jack. I don't want my pants to rip."

It's my turn to roll my eyes. "Maisey, I'm a fireman, okay? I need you to trust me."

The look this woman gives me is intense and questioning. She waivers for a moment but finally gives in and stands back up, ready to try once more.

Moving back into position, I wrap my arms around her upper thighs. Testing the waters, I give her body a gentle tug to see if I can slide her out, and when I do I catch that scent of watermelon again and suddenly Harry Styles and his love of watermelon sugar makes sense to me.

"Wait." Maisey's hands claw into my shoulders. "Something's ripping."

I loosen my grip, slowly walking us back closer to the sleigh to alleviate any tension.

"No, wait." Maisey grunts over my shoulder. "I think it's out... How in the world did I get this tangled on a seat?"

"Things we can discuss after we get you out of this." Bracing myself, I step back and hug her thighs again. "I'm going to give you a big tug now; when I do, I want you to pull your leg as hard as you can."

"But..."

"If they rip, they rip. In fact, if they do I'll buy you a new pair of pants. Deal?"

"Fine," she sighs, finally giving in. "Do what you need to, just get me out."

There is a satisfaction one feels when they do certain things in life. When you can cross items off your to-do list, or get all of the laundry done in one day. My satisfaction comes in the summer when I'm weeding Gran's garden for her.

Pulling a weed out of the ground roots and all is, simply put, thrilling. Tugging on Maisey, I'm envisioning this same kind of immense satisfaction once I get her out—roots and all. The last two times we tried it felt like her pants might come free from their prison, but I want to make sure this time we get her out. Counting to three, I close my eyes and give one last lift-and-pull with all I can muster.

I lift her body easily, but when I pull back, Maisey decides to help me—by throwing herself at me with all of her might. What she doesn't realize is that I'm in no position to take the brunt of her weight as she hits me.

My knees buckle and the air is knocked from my lungs. Snow crunches against my backside and there's a rush of cold as its wet seeps past some of my layers, hitting my skin. When I can finally focus my eyes again, there's one insane woman spread across me. She's laughing so hard she's crying, and I'm spitting out bits of fake snow and pieces of Maisey's hair.

Pushing herself up on her elbows so she hovers above me, her nose only mere inches from mine, Maisey tucks a strand of hair behind an ear and grins, her lips glistening. "So that's how you firemen do it, huh?"

There's a bruise forming...on my ego. "It's usually a bit more coordinated than that."

She leans in closer. "I would hope so, because if that was a rescue, I think you need more training."

My hands fly to her sides, my fingers finding their intended and digging in. When Maisey screams with laughter, bucking herself from my body and into the snow, I take the opportunity. I quickly hop up and pin her down, holding her arms while she giggles. "So, did your pants rip?"

"No," she says as she laughs. It's an infectious laugh and one I don't think I've ever heard from her in all the time I've known her. It's like hearing a new song, and now that I've heard it, it's the best song ever. I hope it gets stuck in my head on repeat. "No ripping, so you did your fire-job."

"My fire-job?" Holding up my hands in front of her face, I wiggle my fingers. "Do you need another round of the ticklers?"

"No." Her eyes widen and she shakes her head back and forth. "I do not. Truce?"

I want to say no to this truce because I'm enjoying rolling around in the snow with this woman. A quick glance up reminds me of our surroundings, and our antics have definitely gotten some attention. A few passersby have stopped to watch us, which is my cue to get us up and out of here. Plus, since I'm just getting started on my apology tour with her, I don't want to blow it.

"Fine, truce." Hopping to my feet, I pull Maisey up with me, only to bring her up so fast our noses slam into each other's, my lips skim her cheek, and hers graze my jaw and neck, leaving a red-hot streak across my flesh in their wake. I'm still processing what's happened when I turn around to find Santa-driver standing on the sidewalk putting his cell phone away and tapping his watch.

"Eileen texted to remind me that I need to have you two back before five. So I'll see you back here at four-thirty." He winks, pointing at the two of us. "You two be good now, and don't get into trouble. Or I'll make sure you get coal in your stockings."

As he walks away, I turn and find Maisey watching me with this weird look on her face. The afternoon sun glistens off her sandy-blonde hair, and her eyes do that thing they do where I swear she's looking into my soul and reading my thoughts.

Someone needs to let Santa know to make sure he's got plenty of coal for this guy—I'm undoubtedly in so much trouble with this woman.

CHAPTER 9

Maisey

Jack McCoy almost kissed me.

I'm fighting nerves, pacing the elevator alone on my way down to the lobby for our interview with the local television station. Thank goodness the elevator has a mirror on one of the walls giving me a second chance to make sure my hair looks okay and that I didn't pick the wrong outfit. All I can think about is the near miss that almost was.

My head still spins from the brush of his lips on my skin earlier. Okay, so maybe there wasn't a full brushing, but at least a close exfoliation of the skin. And maybe it wasn't because he necessarily wanted to kiss me, but...

Why am I thinking of Jack McCoy like this? And why now?

I could tell myself I'm only thinking about him because I'm in character for the role we're playing here, because why admit I'm having fun? Why can't I simply admit that the heat of that man's body so close to mine is a little bit hot mixed with a little bit electric, and that I am quivering inside because I feel like I've been tossed in a blender? A blender of confusion. Confuse, blend, repeat. There's a recipe I can follow for a Friday night special.

The elevator bell dings, signaling my arrival on the lobby floor. As the elevator doors slide open, I'm surprised to find Jack standing on the other side of them.

"Excuse me, miss." Jack steps back and waits for me to exit. I love the moment he does a double take when he realizes it's me. His eyes widen as he skims my figure. Cue my epic redemption after falling from the sleigh.

"Wow. That is a great skirt." A flicker of what I assume to be appraisal dances in his eyes.

"I was hoping for a good reaction." I spin in a circle, twirling so the pleated skirt I'm wearing can do its thing. "Like it?"

"It looks beautiful on you," he murmurs, his voice low and gravelly so only I can hear.

Oh my gosh. This man. The more I'm around him, the more my walls crumble and I'm not even sure why I was so upset with him in the first place. When my eyes slam into his, my stomach feels like a cocktail mixer, the kind a bartender shakes with all his might.

Nervous and unsure of what to do with my hands, I smooth my top and then focus on fiddling with the pleats once the smoothing is done.

"Thank you." I point to the elevator doors as they close. "Where were you going?"

"To find you." Jack points across the lobby to a couch and a couple of old rocking chairs by the grand fireplace. Two giant stage lights illuminate the space, and a few people mill about looking at their watches, probably waiting for me. "Their public relations team is set up and ready to do this."

Taking a deep breath, I close my eyes, channeling my inner Lady Mary. As a once devoted fan of Downton Abbey, I always marveled at the stoic strength and wit Lady Mary managed to carry no matter what situation she faced. I need me some of that right now.

Exhaling, I open my eyes to find Jack watching me and my breath hitches. Jack holds out his hand, taking mine and giving it a squeeze.

"As of now, we're so in love that we're all but vomiting sugar. Got it?"

"Let's do this." I squeeze back. "How bad can it be?"

* * *

Real Bad. That's how bad it can be.

The whole interview is nothing but awkward. In all of my infinite wisdom, the one thing I hadn't thought of doing was to actually get to know Jack more.

When we sat down with Eileen—or "the viper" as I like to call her now—she'd chosen to channel someone, too, only her inner self is channeling someone from the Supreme Court of the United States.

"How did you meet?"

"How did he propose?"

"What's her favorite color?"

"Did Jack have a childhood pet?"

"What's Maisey's favorite meal?"

"Does he do anything that annoys you?"

"Will your wedding be traditional, bohemian, or more of a modern day vibe?"

"What is the first Christmas tradition you'll instill in your children?"

And there it is. The question that makes me crazy.

Out of all the things this woman and her team thought of to ask us, this one question is my bump. No sooner are the words out of her mouth, and my hand is in the air. "Hang on, Eileen. Who said we're having kids?"

Beside me, Jack shifts in his seat and mutters something

about me not going there. It's like he can sense something brewing inside of me—and he isn't wrong.

Eileen points to the legal pad in her lap. "These questions are a version of ones we ask couples who are planning a wedding with us. They help us see how much they know one another, give us insight into their personality, and..."

"They're nosy is what they are, Eileen." I sit back and cross my arms. I'm most certainly a pot on a low boil right now, so someone should let Eileen know she'd better not turn up the heat. "Not everyone can have kids or even wants them, for that matter."

Jack reaches over, squeezing my forearm. "It's just a question, Maisey."

"Is it?" I focus on Eileen. "Seriously, I'm asking why you or anyone on staff would think that question is appropriate to ask a newly engaged couple...or anyone, really."

Eileen throws her hand in the air, in what feels like a flippant move on her part, as if she's brushing my question away. "Like Jack said, it's a question. It's for fun."

Turning to Jack, I look for backup. He may have irked me the last few months, but he's here and while he's here, there is an unwritten expectancy for him to be my wingman. But instead of soothing me or coming to my aid, I watch as his lips form the words "calm down."

Has anyone in the history of calming down ever calmed down when someone has told them, in the heat of the moment THANK YOU VERY MUCH, to calm down?

No.

"There is absolutely nothing about that question that is, to me and probably to a lot of other women out there, fun." Uncrossing my arms, I lean forward, crossing my legs now and sitting on the couch like I'm a guest on Oprah. "When people assume you want something or they think because it's ingrained in us to get married and have a family that every bride is rushing off to do just that, it's so flipping annoying. And guess what? I'm not alone with this way of thinking. I have so many friends who, upon getting married, end up fielding questions as soon as the wedding reception begins about when they're having kids."

Nonplussed, Eileen tilts her head to one side and studies me. "Like we said, it's just a question. I was asked the same thing when I got married. I think when we announced we were engaged people asked me if we were having kids at the engagement party. However, it is an annoying question, I'll give you that."

"Well, that's your experience, Eileen." That low boil turns into a rolling boil, and fast, and I can't seem to dial it down. "Let me ask you this. Do you have kids?"

It's Eileen's turn to fold her arms in front of her chest. "I do."

"Okay, so you're able to have children." Standing up, I take off the mic clipped to the lapel of my top. "A lot of people can't. So for them, it's not only an annoying question, but it's also intrusive and a reminder of what they'll never experience. Other women are choosing not to have kids and it's for their own reasons. Health, career paths, climate change...who cares? It's their choice. I mean, I have a friend who admits she didn't want to have kids because she wanted to only have to take care of herself. Does that make her selfish?"

"I don't think she said anything about being selfish." Jack wraps his hand around mine, but I won't be tethered.

"It's not the point I'm making, Jack." As I pull my hand from his, I realize we're partially in the dark. At some point during my soliloquy, the lights had been turned off and the cameraman stopped filming. "I want Eileen to understand that not every woman needs to be asked if they want to have kids or if they are planning on it. We're engaged and she's asking if we're going to have kids, and we've not even decided on a wedding date. Why do people think they can ask questions like this? It's not anyone's business. Period."

The fact that Jack's eyes start to twinkle as soon as I say "we're engaged" doesn't slip past me. But neither does the look that follows, the one that tells me he does have my back and that he's here for one thing and one thing only.

Me.

Eileen sits gripping her notepad as Jack's hand slides around mine, again, and he stands beside me. With one swift move, he takes off his mic with his free hand and holds it up in the air for all of us to see.

"Well, you heard my gorgeous wife-to-be. We're done here, Eileen. I'm taking this amazing woman to dinner, and if you need us any further, we'll be happy to talk to you tomorrow." Taking my mic from the grip of my other hand, he hands them both to Eileen who still sits unmoving, except for her eyes which follow every move we make. Jack starts walking away, squeezing my hand and pulling me closer to his body as he does. Instinctively, I allow myself to be pulled into his protective embrace as he wraps an arm around my shoulders.

The hotel restaurant is across the lobby. Once we sit down, we look across at each other, and I swear we're both a little paler. I know there's slight horror etched on my face, but wow, the shock and awe on his is epic.

"That was..." I start.

He swallows. "...a train wreck."

"Inside a dumpster fire." My head bobs up and down in agreement.

Jack's brow furrows. "Next to a circus of ridiculous proportions."

"And boy, do I hate clowns." I really do, and at this moment, I feel like one. "Jack, I am so sorry. I cannot believe the verbal vomit that just exploded all over the lobby."

"Do not even apologize, Maisey. Not one bit." Shaking his

head, he reaches across the table for my hand. While this hand-holding thing is quickly becoming a habit I'm not mad at tonight, I must remember we don't feel feelings for Jack McCoy.

"I need to, though. I got crazy for a second but, man, she really hit one of my triggers." I sit back, letting my body succumb to the plushness of the chair. "These chairs are insane. I might fall asleep here before dinner comes."

Jack grins. "They are pretty luxurious."

A waiter comes by to fill our water glasses and tell us the specials, giving me reprieve and a moment to gather my thoughts. It's not like I planned to go off like I did, but it happened and I can't take it back now.

As soon as the waiter leaves us to peruse our menus alone, Jack puts his down and taps my hand. "Can I ask you something?"

Placing my menu on the table, I smooth the tablecloth nervously. I'm a nervous smoother. What can I say? "As long as any questions you ask are not about the last ten minutes, then yes."

Jack's mouth opens, then it closes. It opens again, but this time he grabs his glass of water and takes a drink, eyeing me as he does. When it doesn't look like he's going to actually ask me anything, I pick up my menu and go back to studying it again.

"Well," Jack mumbles, clearing his throat. "It's not necessarily about the last ten minutes, but it is in relation to the subject."

Placing my menu back on the table, I clasp my hands together in front of me. "Please, ask away."

"Do you promise not to get mad?"

I place a hand on my heart. "Swear to the universe and beyond."

"Where did all of that come from?"

"Personal experience." I scoot my chair closer to the table, leaning on my elbows. "I was engaged a long time ago, when I lived in San Francisco. One of the reasons we broke up was because we couldn't see eye to eye on how to raise kids, if we were going to have them in the future. And that was part of the issue for us."

Jack tilts his head to one side. "Because of kids?"

"At the time, I wanted them. During our dating phase and courtship, I guess you could call it, he did, too. Or at least he said he did. It's ironic, but it was a wedding planner who asked us if we were having kids that started the conversation."

"The conversation?"

"The one where he broke up with me because he had realized he didn't want them."

"Oh, Maisey," Jack interrupts, but I'm not done.

"It's not only that he didn't want them. He didn't want them with me." My eyes fill with tears. Tears I hoped wouldn't come right now, but here they are. "However, it's not all sad news. Our breakup ended up being a blessing in disguise."

"Why do you say that?" Jack asks.

"The day we ended my mom called and asked if I ever thought I might move back home. She told me she wanted to bring me in as a partner for the Red Bird, but she left out the fact she'd been diagnosed with early-onset Alzheimer's."

"That's why you moved back to Lake Lorelei?"

"It was the timing. I probably wouldn't have ever said yes to coming back if we hadn't broken up that day. I was so distraught. I felt like I wasn't enough, I second-guessed everything I thought I knew about me, and it all sucked."

Inhaling deeply, I let myself fall back into the safety of the extreme seat cushion once more. "Moving back home gave me the chance to clear my head, get a new perspective, and put that man and his bad attitude far behind me."

"I can understand that. It helps to look at things in hindsight, once you're removed."

"Exactly. My mom helped me change my perspective, and my friend Ari was there, too, as was my niece, Freya. Those girls would organize slumber parties and nights out and activities to keep me busy, and Mom just kept me on my toes."

Jack watches me, his eyes reflecting my emotions implicitly. Oh, this man.

Even though there was no follow-through after he canceled, and even though I have stewed in my own sauces over it, probably for too long at this point, there's still something about him. The way he took control of that situation, taking my hand and steering me away from Eileen. Could it be part of the act, keeping up appearances and all that jazz? Maybe. But for some twisted reason, I'm secretly wishing it's not.

I need to figure out what it is that keeps bringing me back to Jack McCoy.

CHAPTER 10

Jack

For the last ten minutes, I've watched Maisey struggle with the sleeper sofa. Based on the heaviness of our conversation at dinner, I made a choice to sit back and let her do her type A thing here. She needs some time to work off her energy after going off on Eileen.

From where I sat, Eileen deserved every bit of what Maisey gave her. I've always thought that questioning anyone about having kids was like lighting a live fuse, and when I heard Maisey's reasons why she felt so strongly about it, I would have to be a right idiot to not get behind her.

Plus, my own sister. My twin. She can't have kids and I know firsthand what she went through mentally when she got the news. When it comes to handling Eileen, points are on the board for Maisey. However, the same cannot be said for the couch.

"I give up!" Maisey drops the metal bed frame she's been attempting to free from its prison inside the sofa. "This thing is jammed and won't come out."

"Let me try." Flexing my biceps, on purpose, I strut past

Maisey slowly, only stopping to flex again and throw a wink her way.

"You can have at it, Muscles McCoy. I give up." She disappears into the bathroom to brush her teeth and leaves me alone with the sofa. Figuring this will be a piece of cake, I give it a few pulls myself and...nothing. I try adjusting the frame before grabbing the handle and tugging again, but the bed won't come out of the compartment.

A realization washes over me: I won't be sleeping on the pull-out bed tonight. With the sofa being a two-seater, there's the small issue of fitting my body on the couch. A quick glance tells me it's going to be a tight fit, and I could be in for a very sleepless night.

Grabbing a pillow, I lay down on the couch but, as I thought, my feet dangle over the end and my neck is cramped, forced to bend at an extreme angle. I could throw some pillows on the floor and try sleeping there, but I make the choice to stay here for now and grab a throw blanket.

Maisey comes back into the room and stands beside the bed, fluffing her pillows. "Are you really sleeping like that?"

I would shrug my shoulders if I could move them. "I couldn't get it to open, either."

"Oh." She hops into her comfortable and luxurious king-size bed, snuggling under the cloud-like comforter. "You know, I can call the front desk and ask about a rollaway."

A metal rod pokes my spine, but I sit up, grit my teeth, and smile. "It's fine. I'm sure I'll fall asleep quickly. It's been a long day."

Maisey sits in bed, a pile of pillows and blankets surrounding her. The light from her bedside table gives her an ethereal look. Her hair is piled high on the top of her head, her neck exposed as she cocks her to one side and smiles at me.

"Okay." Maisey reaches her hand out toward the lamp on

her bedside table, and I lay my head back down on my pillow. "Thank you, Jack."

And I'm up again. "For what?"

"For coming with me, even though I've been relentless. A relentless reminder that you didn't call. Tonight you had my back. So, thank you."

"You're welcome, Maisey. Good night."

"Night, Jack."

The lamp clicks as she turns it off, and we lay in the darkness, her breath the only sound in the room. Alone, kind of, in the darkness, I hit playback in my mind to go over our time together today leading up to dinner. Turning over in my sausage-like quarters, a giant smile begins creeping across my face. I've gotten to know more about Maisey Montgomery in the last twelve hours than after more than twelve months in the same town. I feel like that's winning.

A sudden pain shoots up my leg, a cramp takes over the right side of my body and causes me to leap to my feet and stifle a scream. The room floods with light as Maisey shoots up in bed.

"What's going on?

"Cramp...ing." I barely manage the words through gritted teeth as I roughly massage my right leg. It's all over in a matter of seconds, but they're painful seconds that pass for me like hours.

As the pain lessens, I breathe out slowly and lower myself back down to the couch.

"What happened, Jack, you okay?

"I can't have a lot of salt." I shrug sheepishly. "Health reasons due to blood pressure, and so I cramp. Suddenly and painfully sometimes."

"Oh wow." Maisey stacks a few pillows behind her against her headboard so she can lean back on them. "Has it happened when you're at work?"

"Oh yeah." I chuckle. "On a ladder. My whole right side started to cramp. I had to get down, though thankfully I wasn't that far up when it happened."

"What caused it to start now?" She inclines her head toward my bed for the night. "Is that couch the culprit?"

Looking at my feet hanging over the edge, I then turn my head toward Maisey and cross my eyes. "What makes you say that?"

"Come on, sleep up here." Before I protest, she's out of bed and grabbing stray pillows from around the room, then uses them to make a small wall in the middle of the bed. "This bed is ridiculously cozy and I can't in my right mind and good conscious sleep here knowing you're one step away from a cramp-seizure-thing."

She tosses the last pillow on the pile and stands with her hands on her hips. "There. It's not perfect, but we'll each have our own space for the night."

"Thanks, Maisey," I say, pulling back the covers and climbing under the sheets. The ridiculously soft sheets which must be made by angels in heaven. "Oh my god. Is this Egyptian cotton?"

"I'm not even sure what that is, much less what Egyptian cotton feels like," Maisey retorts with a laugh. "But it's nice, isn't it?"

Swiveling my head in her direction, I wiggle my eyebrows and mime my eyes rolling back to the back of my head. "Oh, yeah."

Cracking up, she puts her hand back on the bedside lamp. "Good night, Jack."

"Good night." Giving her a mock salute, I throw myself into the comfort of this bed, ready for sleep. But something else knocks at my heart.

I roll over toward the wall of pillows, knowing Maisey is

just on the other side. "Hey, Maisey. Can I ask you something?"

"Of course."

"Why here? Why did you want to come to here so badly and why this year?"

"When I was a little girl, my mom would bring us here. It's a tradition, and it was one she carried on from her mother. No matter what, we would come to the Mistletoe Lodge for the Christmas tour every holiday season, same as she did when she was growing up."

"Was there a specific reason why?"

"No, it's just what we did. We'd go to high tea, we'd look around and maybe go shopping, but we always ended the day at the art gallery."

"Always?"

"Yep." Maisey giggles. "You know, it got to a point that there was this one security guard who kind of knew us, I think."

"What do you mean?"

"It's been so long since I've been here, but from what I remember, there were a few years we would come and the same guy was working the art gallery. He was always super friendly, and in some ways it felt like he knew us, but it I'm sure it was just that he worked here and we came every year."

"A tradition, is a tradition, is a tradition. Maybe for him, it wasn't really Christmas until he saw your mom visiting the gallery."

"Huh. I never thought of it like that." We stay like this for a few moments of silence before Maisey clears her throat. "So, how are you liking Lake Lorelei now that you've been living there for a bit? It's nothing like the fast pace you would have had in Washington D.C. so I'm sure you had some adjustments."

"There's been adjustments, but they've been welcomed."

"Why is that?"

"Well, when I was in D.C. I had been a firefighter for a long time before I was promoted out of active duty there. I took a job working on the arson investigation team for the District of Columbia."

"That would have been intense."

"It was." One day I'll tell her about the families that haunt me still to this day or the times we weren't able to find out who was responsible, but not now. "It was my stint with the team that made me want to take a step back, go back to being on the ground and on the front line with a station. When my grandmother heard Lake Lorelei had an opening, I jumped at the chance."

Maisey laughs out loud. "I love that your grandmother told you about the job."

"Yeah, she's awesome. She's getting older, of course, and my mom had been thinking of moving down here. When I got the job, she was happy I'd be here and able to help Grandmom out—it also lets her off the hook for now."

"You didn't want your mother to move to Lake Lorelei?"

"My mom has had a lot of heartache in her lifetime. My dad was a fireman. He was killed in the line of duty when I was little."

The bed shakes; from the way it moves it feels like Maisey's sat up on her side. "Oh, I'm sorry."

"It was a long time ago. It still hurts a little, especially at the holidays. I want my mom to be happy and to do things for herself. She had to take the role of both parents when he died, and when she was thinking of moving her life back to North Carolina, I don't recall seeing her thrilled about it. Not that she doesn't love her mother..."

"...but picking up your own life to move home for a parent is a big deal." I hear the understanding in Maisey's voice. "I get it."

"Yeah, it is." My feelings bubble beneath the surface, threatening to rise. Time to change the subject. "I know this is going to seem inappropriate now, but I gotta ask...after all that happened earlier and all that happened to you with that jerk you were engaged to back in San Francisco, do you still want kids?"

Maisey's laugh is loud, raucous, and infectious. It's also just what the doctor ordered at this very moment because it lifts the heavy mood in the room.

"Yes, I do. I made a deal with myself, though, to not expect it in the package I think it should come in."

Now she's got me curious. "What do you mean?"

"I'm going to have kids the best way I can for me. It will look like what I need it to look like. If I'm so lucky that I can have my own, that's going to be awesome. If I'm married when I do it, even better. But if I can't have kids or I don't get married, and I choose to adopt, then that's what I'll do." She lets out a giant sigh. "Essentially I gave myself permission to become a parent the way I'm supposed to, and I'm not going to try to force it. The end. Thank you for coming to my TED talk."

I prop myself up on one elbow, placing my head in the palm of my hand. "Being a parent is different for everyone. My sister's a pet parent. She's a single mom to two cute Yorkie terriers. She also can't have children, so she would have appreciated your words tonight. It's always been a pain point for her as well."

"Really? Wow, thanks, Jack. I have friends who are in the same boat. I hurt for them and wish I could do more."

"I think what you did was perfect."

We sit in more silence with the darkness around us. Running my fingers along the pillows, I fight the urge to pull one away. Every particle of my body is drawn to Maisey. As it has always been and, coming on this trip, I feel it even more.

I sit and stew with my feelings, while beside me the sheets rustle and a soft thud tells me Maisey's lain down again.

"I'm going to try to sleep now," she whispers. "Good night."

"Night, Maisey." Tapping the pillow softly, I roll over on my side and turn my back to her, only to roll right back over so I'm facing in her direction again.

Because Maisey is one woman I never want to turn my back on. Ever.

CHAPTER 11

Maisey

Sleep didn't come easy last night. I guess having a distraction like Jack lying next to me could be one reason, another reason would be the adrenaline rush from telling Eileen my mind—but I think I'm just excited. Joyful. Riddled with electricity, if one can be riddled with that.

Today is the private art gallery viewing and I'm over the moon.

I'm still in bed, stifling a yawn and wishing I could magically call a cup of coffee to my hand Harry Potter-style, when there's a soft knock at the door out in the main room of the suite. When there's no movement next to me, I pull a few pillows down, expecting to see Jack asleep on his side of the wall, only he isn't.

Closing my eyes, I wait a few beats, assuming he's in the living room so of course he'll answer the door. But the knock is back, only this time it's louder. That's when I notice the sound of what could be water hitting a wall—he must be in the shower.

I roll out of bed, stumbling out into the living room.

When I get to the door, the repetitive cadence starts again, but I manage to open the door on the third rap. Theo stands before me with what I think could be described as a tight smile, and beside him is a cart filled with coffee, juice, and an assortment of covered plates.

"Morning, ma'am. Breakfast for you and Mr. McCoy. Shall I wheel it inside?"

"Nah." I take the handle of the cart and pull it through the doorway. "I can take it from here, Theo. Thank you."

Theo nods his head curtly and bows once at the waist before he disappears back down the corridor, leaving me alone to roll this bad boy inside. By the time Jack finally exits the bathroom, I've set up our feast and have transformed the dining room table with all of the goodies.

Hearing the door open to the master suite, I swing around, sweeping my hand out and across the food. "I bet you smelled breakfast...ta da. Food and caffeine is here."

Only, as I turn around, I'm the one who is drooling.

Jack stands in the doorway with one very lucky towel cinched around his waist, his hair still wet and droplets of water spilling down his chest. My eyes are hypnotized when one stray drop begins a serious journey, headed south, going where no woman has gone...

"Maisey? Are you listening?

"Yes. Of course." I snap back to attention, plastering a fake smile across my face because of course I was not listening. I'm too busy riding a white water rapid down Jack's six pack. "I'm distracted. All of the excitement. You know. Art gallery today!"

"Ah." That smile of his is back. It's perfect and charming, and when he shares it with me I feel like I'm in on a secret. A secret he's telling only me, and it's ours to keep. He jerks a thumb over his shoulder. "Give me a few seconds, I'll get dressed."

Thank the heavens he manages to find his clothes before he comes back to the table. Jack pulls out a chair, parking that cute butt of his in it as he grabs a croissant and butters it, then pours his coffee. Almost as an afterthought, Jack hops up and goes around to the other side of the table, where the cart sits, and starts poking around it.

"Is there any jelly or marmalade?" Holding up his croissant, he gives me a sad face. "I need something on this."

"I thought I saw some over there somewhere." Scanning the cart, I can't see any. My eyes skip across the dining table to the butler's chest against the wall. Success. I point for Jack to see. "There. I see a few jars over there in that basket."

"Good spotting." Jack looks in the basket and grabs a jar with a giant strawberry on the side of it. "Something about strawberry jelly that I just dig, you know?"

"Actually, yes." Laughing, I put my cup down and lean in to grab one of the small quiche bites piled on a plate. "Strawberries are one of my favorite fruit pies to make. Always popular, too. But it's lemon meringue that I really love to eat when it's a special occasion."

"I've had your lemon meringue pie. Out of this world." Jack flicks the spread around the croissant with a knife before taking a bite. "Mmm. This is good, but it can't compete with your strawberry tarts..."

My hand flies to my forehead. "Stop it with the compliments, Jack. Someone will mistake us for two people who like each other."

"But that's the thing." Jack stops chewing. "I do like you, Maisey."

Everything stops. I'm sure he means to say those words in the kind of way one tries to express themselves to a friend, or a fr-enemy since that's what I think we're graduating from? But the waters are muddy now from this trip and all of the bonding talk we're having.

It's all too much for me to even think about today, I just want to go to see the art exhibit and walk in my mom's footsteps. That's all. I don't want to be thinking about making up with Jack, or the fact that I am feeling feelings for him. No.

But I am. Feeling feelings, that is. A rush of them, in fact. I drag my eyes from my plate, where I've been dicing up my tiny quiche for the last thirty seconds, seeking Jack's eyes, but it's not his eyes that keep my attention. It's his lips. His full, giant swollen lips. Oh, wow. They look painful.

"Hey." I put my fork down, touching my lips before indicating to his mouth. "Something is up. You okay?"

Jack rubs his lips together and his eyes grow wide. His hand flies to his mouth while he starts clicking his tongue against its roof, his head turning to face me, eyes bulging even further as he does. He points to his lips. "I can't fee my moooww."

"You can't feel your...mouth?"

Jack nods and keeps pointing to his lips. "My mooowww is nummm. I can't fee it." Licking his lips, he sits scratching his head with his brow furrowed in worry.

Being in the food industry, I feel like I've seen this kind of reaction before. I lean over and swipe the strawberry jam jar from its spot in front of him. "Are you allergic to anything?"

Jack nods. "Bee stings."

"Nothing else?"

"No." Jack pushes his chair away from the table and is standing now, pointing to the jar. "What's in it?"

A quick inspection of the jar tells us what we need to know. "It has raw honey in it, Jack, so your allergy could have been set off from this delightful treasure of local artisan jam."

Holding up a finger, telling me to wait a minute, Jack sprints out of the room. He's back a second later holding an EpiPen in his hand, his face washed in relief. The smile he wears tells me its healing powers are already at work.

Breathless, I sit back hard in my chair. "Did that really just happen?"

* * *

The lobby is busier today than it had been when we arrived yesterday. A large family crowds around the giant fireplace snapping photos by the Christmas tree, and a pianist tickles the ivories and plays all of the old favorites of the holiday season.

Turning to Jack, I stand on tiptoes and inspect his lips. "Swelling going down?"

"Feels like it." Jack runs his fingers across his lips, taking a moment to tap each one. "Not as bad as before, that's for sure. I can form words now, but for a second there I thought my lips were paralyzed for life."

"Well, they weren't, so we dodged a bullet and"—I clap my hands together with glee—"in the Saint Nick of time, too. It's time for our gallery tour."

"Well, it looks like you two are having a nice start to your morning." I look up in time to find Eileen waving at us as she crosses the lobby. "Did you two sleep well?"

Jack and I exchange a look of knowing, and I nod. "We did, thank you."

"I'm glad I caught you both." Eileen clasps her hands in front of her, her usual controlled demeanor nowhere in sight. "I wanted to say I'm sorry about yesterday. I could have handled it better and I didn't. I want you to know, Maisey, that I took your feedback to our marketing department and your words were heard."

"Oh?" I ask.

"Moving forward, we'll be asking more inclusive questions and less personal ones of our couples." Eileen shrugs as she shifts her weight from one foot to the other. "None of us had ever had anyone share those other perspectives with us before, and I'm glad you spoke up. We won't be using any of the footage from yesterday for our campaigns, obviously. In fact, you won't have to do an interview with us at all."

"Really?" I'm fairly certain my face lights up when she says this. A load of weight lifts from my shoulders.

"Nope. No interview. We've changed a few things around." Eileen whips out her phone and pulls up a new itinerary for us. "Unfortunately, the art gallery has to be closed for the day, so we had to move a few things and replace that part of the tour."

"Oh." I try to hide my disappointment, but there's no way I can. My whole body physically reacts to Eileen's news.

"You okay?" Jack asks as he wraps an arm around me. I want to make a mental note and let him know later how well timed that arm snuggle is, but I have no bandwidth for it right now. I'm too disappointed.

"I was really looking forward to the tour." I turn my attention back to Eileen. "Will we get to do it later?"

"We should be able to squeeze it in tomorrow before you go. We've been understaffed here this year, which is part of the problem, so I do apologize. But"—her green eyes flash with excitement—"I think you're going to love what we have planned now."

Crossing my fingers, I hold them in the air in a show of excited faith as I try to ignore the chuckle Jack swallows when I do so.

Eileen's eyes bounce back and forth between Jack and I, gauging our interest. "I think you mentioned in your essay the two of you liked spending your weekends out on the family ranch riding?"

"Did I say that?" Gulping, I don't dare look in Jack's direction. I feel the shift in his energy like nobody's business.

"I was in such a hurry to write my essay, I keep forgetting what I put in it."

"I was worried she wasn't going to tell you about her hidden talent," Jack suddenly interjects, pulling me in even closer. His grip is vise-like. Methinks he may be irked with me. "I bet Maisey didn't tell you she's known as the female version of Roy Rogers around Lake Lorelei."

I'm going to kill him.

"Stop that—you're deflecting, honey." Leaning in, I grab Eileen's arm and pull her nearer to where I stand. "Jack used to compete on the rodeo circuit."

Eileen's eyes light up. "That is amazing! I had a feeling you two were going to love a horseback ride around the estate this morning."

Lucky for me, I know how to ride. I can't say the same thing about my travel companion, though. "We're going to have a blast."

"Oh yay!" Eileen squeals. "We'll have two of our best horses ready for you soon. Dress warmly, it's chilly out there today, and keep an eye out, you never know when you may see an elf."

Watching her trot off, I'm at once curious why elves would be wandering the Mistletoe Lodge and also buoyed with a sense of accomplishment as I see a bead of sweat forming on Jack's upper lip.

"Maisey, I told you horseback riding is not in my wheelhouse. What did you do that for?"

"I'm sorry." I wave a hand in front of me, flustered. "I get caught up in the moment and I can't stop myself."

"Well, luckily I can kind of ride a horse," he grumbles, touching his lips. "I can't even defend myself properly because my lips are still half asleep and here you are, volunteering me to do pony tricks. Jeez—what happened to the woman who was lying in bed thanking me last night?"

There's a small group of tourists standing nearby, and a few of their heads almost swivel off their necks and land on the floor beside us. Feeling a heat rush to my cheeks, I grab Jack's arm and steer him out of the center of the lobby.

"You need to pipe down." Looking around, I see Eileen chatting with the concierge, who takes off in a mad sprint a moment later. When she sees me and gives me a thumbs-up, I take it as our signal that the horses are on the way. Giddy up.

Jack pulls out his cell phone and flicks through his apps. This simple act reminds me I need to check in with the Red Bird. "Do you have cell service down here?"

He shakes his head. "I haven't had good reception since we got here. You may want to use the phone back in the room."

"Okay." I shuffle my feet and lean against the wall, zipping my jacket up tight to my neck. "I'm glad I wore this, especially since we're not going to do the gallery tour now."

Jack looks up from his phone and winks at me. "Eileen said we'll get to do it tomorrow. I need to see those snow globes, so she'd better come through."

"Ah." That's right. "I forgot your grandmom and your mom will want some pictures, won't they?"

"You bet they will." He chuckles. "But hey, seeing the countryside is just as fun."

Narrowing my eyes playfully, I place one hand on my hip. "Even while riding a horse?"

Jack's face twists from panic to calm, before he reaches out to pat my arm. "I'm joking. I'll be fine. I have ridden before."

"Famous last words." I give him a good-natured swat, chewing back a laugh as he sidesteps my hand. Maisey having fun with Jack is a way nicer person than the Maisey who was mad at Jack. I'm at least laughing a whole lot more. Do I still wonder what happened, why he never called? I guess part of me would like to know, but new Maisey wants to let it go. She wants to have fun, she's at the Mistletoe Lodge, she's having a great time in luxury surroundings, and she's laughing herself senseless.

When I look in Jack's direction and see he's laughing as well, surely I'm not seeing things when his eye catches mine and his gaze changes. It softens at the same time it intensifies, and a rush of heat spreads over my body.

We stand in our corner of the lobby, grinning at each other. Sharing this secret smile of ours at the same moment about the same thing.

And for one fleeting second, I feel what it's like to have Jack McCoy all to myself.

CHAPTER 12

Jack

While I wasn't lying when I said I could ride a horse, I simply left out the part that it's been awhile since I've sat in the saddle. The last time I climbed on and took a ride was about ten years ago. Lucky for me my instincts kicked in today and I wasn't left completely in the dust.

But did I spend the first fifteen minutes on my horse wishing I hadn't gone horseback riding and swearing to myself that Maisey would rue the day she entered this contest? You bet I did. With each bump I hit, every step that horse took when it trotted and cantered, I thought of all the things I wanted to do to her for revenge.

To top it off, our guide, Brent, spent the better part of an hour flirting with Maisey, and even though we're only pretending to be engaged, I'm irked. Does it help my case that he looks like he just rode back in from one of the far pastures of Yellowstone with his cowboy hat high on his head? This guy's spurs even sparkle. Unreal. It's also unreal I'm having FOMO about spurs. It's not like Maisey is doing anything to try and stop the flirting, either.

Not that I can stake any claims here, but come on. We're supposed to be in character.

"It is gorgeous here, Brent." Maisey's breathless and all smiles, holding the reins casually in one hand as she turns her horse, aptly named Daisy, around to face me on my pony. "And when it's this silent? I love it."

The fields are a sight to behold, even if they are covered with fake snow. It's the illusion that does the job for people like Maisey. Even though we're a stone's throw away from the estate, you would never know it. Brent's tour included the whole of the estate grounds, so we'd literally ridden to every corner.

Making our way through a final grouping of trees, I'm in the back trailing Maisey who is right behind Brent. He holds up the branch of a pine tree laden with snow and moves his steed out of the way so Maisey and her horse can pass. "This will make it easier for you to get past. Let's keep your hands on the reins."

Since he first saw Maisey, Brent's pretty much purred like a male cat in heat the whole time we've been out here. Honestly, I would have thought he'd let the act go by now. But nope. This faux fiancé gets no respect.

Maisy clears the branch and I dig my heels into my horse so we can make our way under the tree branch as well. At the same time I duck my head to go underneath it, Brent turns away and lets go of his end. I guess since Maisey made it through, he figures his job is done.

The branch whips down in front of me, giving me no time to react. Thwacking into my chest, it slams into me with the force of a big rig and knocks the wind out of my lungs. My body arches backwards and I lose my grip on the reins, but thankfully I manage to grasp the saddle horn before my body slides off the side of the seat.

Snow creeps down my chest and back, its wetness seeping

into all the possible spots it can when the branch hits me. Teeth chattering, I glance up to look at my companions, certain they're right there, wanting to help. Boy, am I wrong.

Maisey is looking around with joy, Brent watching her. What is this guy even being paid to do anyway?

"Jack, this is stunning." Maisey turns around in her saddle to find me covered in snow. "What...what are you doing?"

Shaking the snow off my head, I tug on the reins to keep my horse still. He's a regal pony named Pokey. Can you guess that Brent picked him out for me? "I needed to cool down, so I decided to run into this tree branch filled with fake snow."

Maisey shoots me a dirty look. "Don't be a scrooge."

"Our artificial snow is made from a plant-based material and is actually good for the environment." Brent winks at Maisey. "It's a first of its kind."

"I'm sure." Giving my body a big shake, I flick snow particles off of my jacket. Glancing ahead, my heart actually skips a beat when I see the stables in front of us. It's signaling this ride is coming to an end, and I'm all for it, but I won't let Brent know that. "Oh man, you guys. Are those the stables already?"

"Do you want to stay out longer?" Maisey asks, turning in her saddle to look in my direction. "I'm down if you and Brent are."

I open my mouth to protest, but luckily Brent finds a way in first. "Sadly, I have another tour I have to take out so we can't continue now."

"That's a bummer." Maisey shrugs her shoulders as she brings Daisy to a stop so she can climb down. "You win some, you lose some."

"But, I can take you out later if you like? You were good out there. I can tell you ride often." Brent is full of good ideas as he leaps off his horse to help Maisey down, ignoring me,

"Thanks." She places her hand in Brent's and lets him

guide her to the ground. "I try to go out at least twice a month."

Noted. She's an avid horseback rider in disguise.

Brent turns to me, only holding a hand out to help me down when he sees my foot is caught in a stirrup. "You were— well, I'm glad we got you back, but you may want to work on your handling skills with your betrothed here. She can help you out."

This guy. I need to get Woody here to back off.

"I guess we need to have a few solo practice runs, right, honey?" Standing behind Maisey, I wrap both arms around her waist and pull her close to my body so I can kiss her cheek. "I respond better to one-on-one, I'm not a fan of group activities."

Playing along, she leans her cheek into my lips before pushing me away with a quick thrust of her hip into mine. "We have to go, Brent, so we can get back to the hotel, but thank you again for a great ride."

Am I a little snarky as we walk away, making sure to put my arm around Maisey's waist and keep it there, snugly, until we're out of Brent's eyesight? You bet I am. Maisey even lets me keep it there until we round a corner and the stables are safely out of sight.

She grabs my hand and flings it off her. "You were a bit possessive just now."

"We're supposed to be engaged, Maisey." I throw my hands in the air. "How does it look if my fiancée is flirting with the stable boy?"

"Me, flirting with him?" She shakes her head and wags a finger in the air. "He was flirting with me."

"There's no difference."

She stops in her tracks. "Oh yes, there is."

"How can you even say that?"

Maisey's eyes narrow. "Because if I'm flirting with someone, they're going to know it."

Now we're getting somewhere. "Have you ever flirted with me?"

"Yes, but we both know what happened after that." Maisey crosses her arms in front of her chest. "It seems my milkshake brought you to the yard, but you decided you wanted a refund."

Every time I think she's let it go, it comes back up. I have no one to be mad at except myself. Now is as good of time as any to pony up, excuse the pun.

"Maisey, you're right. I never called. I'll say I'm sorry for another ten years if I need to, but I'm hoping I don't have to." My throat seizes and my mouth goes dry. The words aren't coming as easily as I need them to. "I'm not the kind of man who disappears or keeps secrets, but this one time in my life I did."

Maisey narrows her eyes as she leans against the exterior brick wall of a bakery, touting a sign proclaiming "Santa's favorite sugar cookies served inside!"

"Go on." She gives one sharp nod of her head. "I'm listening."

Taking a big breath, I continue. "The day after I asked you out, my sister-in-law passed away after fighting cancer for the last two years. I had to leave Wyatt and Freya's wedding early, because that's when my mother called to tell me I was needed back home, in Washington D.C."

"Oh wow." Maisey's face is void of color. She reaches out and takes my hand. "I'm so sorry."

"It hit us all hard, but my brother Liam was a mess." Reaching into my jacket pocket, I pull out my cell phone knowing a visual representation will have more impact. I tap open an app and hold the phone out for Maisey to see. "These are his kids, Vivian and Levi. This was the reason I disappeared and it's the reason I never called."

It's been a few months since I've talked about Kara's death and what it did to our little family dynamic. I can feel the sting of tears behind my eyes, but I push it back with as much force as I can muster.

"Everything shifted and we all had to shift with it. Immediately. These two had just turned three and needed to have stability and security during a time when no one could promise it." Tapping the app closed again, I start to put my phone away, but Maisey's hand reaches out and touches mine.

"Will you show me their photo again?"

I open the app and hand the phone over for inspection. She gazes at the image on the screen in front of her, a soft half-smile on her lips. Her eyes slowly rise up, meeting mine, and she pulls the phone close to her heart.

"They're adorable," she whispers. "And I'm a jerk. I'm sorry, Jack."

Taking the phone back from her outstretched hand, I shrug one shoulder. "How were you to know? The only person who knows about this is Dub and he's not told anyone."

"Why haven't you told anybody about this?"

"We all needed time to grieve and Liam wanted time to figure out what his next steps were." I stare at my feet, crunching fake-snow clumps under my shoe. "He's decided to move here after the New Year. Time for a fresh start for him and the kids, so it's time we all started dealing with it."

Maisey opens her mouth at the same time my phone dings, sending a text message from my sister to my screen.

ETTA: WARNING. THEY'RE INVITING SINGLE WOMEN TO XMAS EVE. THERE IS NO ESCAPE.

My stomach turns a somersault when I read her words. I swear, the women in my life only want to make me crazy, don't they? Knowing my mother and grandmother both are coming from a good place, and both have hearts of gold, is no solace. It makes it harder. Plus, the person I want to bring with me is only starting to really acknowledge me and finally talk to me so there's that.

I'm not able to answer Etta right now, so I put my phone away. Maisey's busy digging around in her purse. I swear her arm is halfway buried in that giant bag of hers.

"Looking for something?"

"Lip balm." She suddenly stops, snapping her hand out of her bag. "Oh wait. I probably shouldn't use it. It's got beeswax in it."

"Why can't you use it? It's not like we're going to make out for hours on end—or are we and you forgot to tell me it's in the contract?"

She laughs. "I don't want to cause any kind of reaction. I can grab another one at the hotel spa when we get back."

"Seriously, Maisey, I don't think it'll be an issue. I'm only mildly allergic and it's not as bad as, say, a peanut allergy where some people can't be in the same room with any kinds of nuts or else they have a reaction."

"Now I can't find it." Maisey shoves her hand back in her bag, pulling items out and placing them in my clutches for me to hold while she digs around. "Now I want to find it so I can throw it away. Better safe than sorry."

She shoves a pack of tissues in my hand, unused, and her wallet. A few seconds later she balances a photograph there as well.

The photo looks like it was taken about fifteen years ago or so. Holding it in the air, I show it to Maisey. "Who's this?"

Her face softens as she reaches out and takes it from me. "Me, my sister, and my mom. This was one of our Christmas trips coming here, to the Mistletoe."

Taking the photo back I inspect it and point out an object

in her mom's hands. "Is she holding a photo? A framed photograph?"

Tilting her head to one side, Maisey leans in and takes a closer look. "Oh wow! She is. I forgot she used to do that."

"This was a thing?"

"Not always, but for a few years it was. My mom brought me and my sister, but like I told you, it was my grandmother who started the tradition. I forgot she would come with us from time to time, but this particular year was the one she'd passed away. So, Mom brought her photo so she could still be part of the tradition."

I hand the picture back to Maisey and watch as she carefully places it in her bag, along with her wallet, tissues, a small makeup kit, and what resembles a sewing kit and deodorant. Are all handbags carrying the same stock as a small pharmacy these days?

I want to know more about her family, to know about their trips here, and why that photo is in her bag, but these are all questions I'll have to save for later. From behind, someone calls our names. When I turn around, Theo marches toward us on a mission, holding a tray with two takeout cups balanced on top of it.

"There you are. I've got the hotel car parked across the street. We have just enough time to get you two back for your couple's massage." He holds the tray out in front of us. "Two hot chocolates, piled high with whipped cream the way the gentleman likes it," he finishes with a wink. I could get used to this.

"You know, I was also going to ask about the treatment." Maisey takes a quick sip of her drink before she continues. "We're booked in for a couple's massage, but we're wondering if we can each have our own treatment instead? It's not that I don't want to share the moment with this fella, but I'm more of a hot stone kind of gal, and this guy loves a good moisturizing facial."

"No can do." Theo holds his hands up in mock surrender, while I consider the fact Maisey thinks my skin needs hydration. "Sorry, but the powers that be etched this weekend in stone and we have to stick with the plan."

"Except for the part where the tour is rescheduled," I make sure to remind him.

"Yes, well, except that, but we're going to make it up to you. A couple's massage can be very romantic. It will be good for the two of you—we have couples tell us all the time how that one hour has reconnected them. You'll love it." Theo jerks his head to where the car is parked. "Come on."

Theo pivots and plods his way back to where the Mistletoe's car sits waiting patiently for us. Beside me, a worried fake bride-to-be is having a panic attack about a couple's massage.

Maisey bites her lip with worry, and instinctively I reach out and grab her hand, pull it to my lips, and kiss it. As soon as my lips hit her skin, her body goes rigid at the same time my heart drops like a lead weight to my tummy.

"I. Uh..." I drop her hand, feeling heat coursing through my veins and flooding my cheeks. "Sorry. I'm definitely in character. Wasn't thinking."

Maisey stares at my hand for a moment before she reaches out and grabs it, wrapping it in hers. "You're right. It's part of the whole weekend package, isn't it?" She winks at me and tugs my hand. "Come on, we're off to the spa. Let's go relax."

Famous last words.

CHAPTER 13

Maisey

After Theo drops us at the spa entrance, Jack and I are escorted to our own separate changing areas, where I mumble a silent prayer of gratitude. After all of the other escapades since we've arrived, there is no way I'm sharing a changing room with him. I'm most certainly not prepared to take my clothes off in front of this man, no matter what he is doing to me physically, and considering I'm still processing what he said earlier, I need a few minutes alone to breathe.

I manage to sneak in a quick shower and get the smell of stables off me. Wrapping up in one of the spa-provided bathrobes, I take a seat in their "Quiet Lounge" with a goal of being quiet. But Jack and his big reveal keep showing up in my thoughts, and I'm not getting any reprieve. I feel like a jerk and even though he says he can forgive me, I still acted like a spoiled brat who didn't get their way. I avoided this man and held a grudge for months, and all because I jumped to a conclusion.

How much time have I wasted in my life by making assumptions and not doing my own follow-through? It's so easy to place blame elsewhere than to hold up a mirror and look at ourselves. I'm lost in life's contemplations and sipping on a hot cup of chamomile tea when one of the spa assistants finds me.

"Maisey?" she asks. When I nod, she flicks her hand, indicating that I follow her. "Come with me."

I follow her through the back hallways, which wind around like a small maze, until we arrive at a large wooden door. A plaque on the wall tells me we've arrived at the Honeymooner's Private VIP Lounge.

The assistant steps back, holding the door open for me to enter. This room has it all: a private jacuzzi that's barely big enough for two, a table with all kinds of fruit scattered across it, a cheese platter with a chocolate fondue fountain, and two massage tables set up side by side. The air smells like cinnamon and vanilla, and the peaceful sounds of a harp cascade through the speakers.

"Wow." Jack is already here and spinning in a circle in the middle of the room, taking it all in. "If I haven't said it yet today, thank you again for bringing me. I don't even know what half of those cheeses are on the table, but I already know I'm going to like them."

Jack steps past me, making his way over to the table while also allowing me to catch a whiff of his scent as he breezes by. I was hoping for a fresh, clean, woodsy odor, but someone, and I'm not naming names, smells like the stable. "Did you want to grab a shower first?"

Jack grabs a plate and piles it high with an assortment of cheeses and special gluten free artisan crackers. "I meant to, but I forgot." Gotta love the charm of a man who is nonplussed by his own stink. "They were rushing me in the changing rooms to get in here. Said they've been running behind today, and apparently we're actually like ten minutes late for our appointment."

"It's not like we could help being late. They're the ones who moved the schedule around."

"You've got me worried now." Jack holds his arm out and promptly aims his nose at his armpit, taking a big whiff. "Do I smell that bad?"

I lean over the table and sniff Jack. "Ooof. Maybe you can at least rinse off before they come?"

The words no sooner leave my mouth when the door to the room opens and our two masseurs, one male and one female, stroll in.

"Well." Jack's eyes meet mine and his brow furrows. He leans in so only I can hear him. "I guess we'll just have to wait it out. Maybe they won't notice."

"I'm Kelly and this is Luke." The female masseuse stands beside Jack and both she and her partner begin changing the sheets in front of us. It's hard not to notice when her nose crinkles and her mouth quirks, like she's trying to hold something in between her teeth. "You're Maisey and Jack, yes?"

"That's right." I nod, watching and waiting...and there it is again. Her nose moves a little bit. She's smelling the air around her, and I think I know why.

"It's nice to meet you both," Luke says over his shoulder as he smooths a sheet over the other table and turns to me. "Are you ready to get up here?"

I nod and wait for him to pull back the thin cotton sheet for me to slide underneath. Now, I've been planning for this moment the past few days, knowing it was coming.

The moment I'm half-naked in the same room as Jack.

When Luke turns his head, I make sure Jack's is turned away, too, before I drop my bathrobe and slide under the sheet like a baseball player coming into home. I almost knock Luke over in the process.

"Whoa, you okay there?" Luke's laugh fills the quiet space. "Thought you were gonna slide off the table for a second."

"I want to keep things a mystery for as long as possible, right, sweetie?" I glance over at Jack and wink. With the sheet tucked around me, I'm feeling more confident already.

"She's a conundrum, wrapped up in a mystery, boxed with a flair of drama, and tied into a pretty bow, this one," Jack says as he settles in on his stomach on the next table.

I stick my tongue out. "Just shush, Jack."

"You're so graceful," he teases, stifling a yawn at the same time.

"Sorry, are we keeping you up?"

"I've been very busy on vacation today." He stretches out, reaching his arms high above his head. This is when Kelly—who has been rocking the most peaceful expression I've ever seen—twists her face, and her nose goes into the air and does that crinkling thing again.

"I'm sorry." She stops and puts a hand to her nose. "For some reason it smells like someone rode a horse through here."

"Oh yeah, that would be Jack." He wants to call me dramatic? We'll see about that. "I should apologize, but my fiancé forgot to shower when we arrived."

Jack shoots daggers in my direction. "You didn't need to throw me under the bus."

"The jig is up." I put my hands in the air. "I think they can smell the bus, sweetie."

"We can," Kelly says quietly. "We can smell the bus."

"Maybe there's a candle you can light?" I look up at Luke, who shares a knowing look with me that says "we've got this" as he strides over to a cabinet, opens the door, and pulls out a giant candle. Situation is now under control for the most part, and within minutes, the room is once again still. It smells like orange and vanilla mixed with horse manure, but it's quiet.

Luke's hands are magic. He finds knots I don't know exist and lulls me into a serene state of mind in no time flat. I'm in a place of relaxation that is usually reserved for those who meditate on a daily basis or are gurus or something, not me. I'm not supposed to be this chill.

Judging by the lawnmower-like snoring coming from the table beside me, Jack's pretty relaxed as well. All is peaceful, so I allow myself to be here and simply enjoy my massage, letting my mind zone out and just be.

Luke's hands dance their way down my back, really working into my muscles, when his fingers skim a sensitive area below my ribs. Luke's fingers have found my spot. It's not just any old spot, but *the* spot. The one that has a release button attached to it where all the drama buried deep inside rises to the top and everyone gets a front row seat.

You see, I'm a ticklish human being. Always have been. When I was little, my sister would sit on me and tickle me to get what she wanted, and she always won. Tickling paralyzes me. I lose all control of limbs, of my voice and its pitch, and I end up promising the tickler in question anything they want in an effort to get away from their evil, prodding digits.

Luke's fingers are like a hot button for me. Everything happens so fast; one minute, I'm enjoying my massage and the next, my body's rigid as my head snaps up from its prone position on the table. I'm lying face-first and can't see what's above me, so of course I don't know Luke just so happens to be standing right above me at the very moment I shoot up like lava from an exploding volcano.

My back arches and my head jerks, connecting with his chin and effectively cracking it open. Luke falls to the ground and cries out in pain, cupping the area of his face where his chin is, blood beginning to seep through his fingers. The sight of blood always makes me faint and this time is no exception, so I throw my head back down on the table—and fast—while the room spins.

"I know first aid." Thank goodness for Jack. He's already off his table and has somehow managed to wrap his sheet around his waist in one swift movement, hiding all of what the good lord and his mama gave him. He inclines his head in Kelly's direction. "Can you please go find me the first aid kit? I know you guys have one here."

With one eye open and the other one closed so the room will stop spinning, I watch Kelly race out the door. I know I feel like I'm pale as a ghost, but she's paler than that, if they have a color for it.

Compressing the wound, Jack's a stoic figure of calm in the middle of the proverbial storm. Kelly runs back in with a small red bag in her hand, shoving it at Jack. "Here. Should I call 911?"

"No." Jack chuckles at the same time Luke manages to lift an arm, holding out his hand to Kelly. "You may want to take him to a doctor nearby, though. Looks like he may need a few stitches to close the wound."

"See?" Luke looks at Kelly. "I'm going to be fine, honey, it was only an accident."

Completely interested in what's happening now, I open both eyes and sit up on the table and watch Kelly as she kneels beside Luke, embracing him.

"Who knew being a masseuse means it's a contact sport?" Kelly shoots a knowing look in my direction as she smiles. "I saw the whole thing and I know it was an accident. Are you okay?"

"I'm fine." Propping myself up on my elbows, I hide my face in my hands. "But I feel terrible. I'm so sorry."

Kelly turns and smiles at Jack as she helps Luke get to his feet. "It's a good thing I had a superhero on my table to help us out. Have you taken a first aid class?"

"Ha." My voice breaks the air, the pride in it surprising even me. "My fiancé is a first responder."

"Then it's my lucky day." Luke puts his hand out to shake Jack's. "Thanks, man."

"You're welcome, but you two should go to a doctor's office now so they can take care of that wound. We can tell the staff what happened. Just go."

Grateful, the couple wrap their arms around one another and head out of the room, while I wrap the sheet tightly around my body.

"See." I hold my arms out wide before wagging a finger at Jack. "I told you this would be relaxing."

CHAPTER 14

Jack

I didn't expect the lobby to be as packed as it is with people, and all for tonight's tree lighting ceremony. It's like trying to swim through a school of fish as I make my way to the comfort of the lounge beyond. Spotting a two-seater couch next to the fireplace, I make a beeline for it and claim it as mine.

After getting Etta's text earlier, I made sure to come down a few minutes ahead of schedule so I can give her a call before Maisey joins me. Reception hasn't been the best in the hotel, but luckily I get a few bars of service by the fireplace. I'm grateful Etta answers on the first ring.

"I had a feeling I'd hear from you sooner rather than later. How are you going to avoid this whole holiday party blind date situation Mom and Gran are prepping for you?"

"They're playing dirty, I can say that. I thought going away this weekend would absolve me of having to deal with their matchmaking, but those two seem to be on a mission this year, huh?"

"More than ever. Hey, at least they leave me alone when they get this focused on you." The upside of being a twin—

you can slink into the background, if needed, when the attention turns to your sibling. Especially when it's about this particular subject.

"Mom goes easy on you because you've got fur babies, and a job that you're married to for now. The day she even gets a hint you're restless, we both know she'll start looking for someone for you, too."

"What did you say? You broke up."

"I said, Mom loves her grand-dogs and watch your back." Okay, maybe I paraphrased.

"Shush, Jack." Etta clicks her tongue in my ear, a signal she's lost in thought. "I've been thinking about this, and the only way for you to deal is to show up and suck it up, or get sick and not come."

"Such great advice," I coo in her ear. "Thanks."

"You can always go out and rent a girlfriend. That'll solve your problem at least for the night."

She's not wrong. When my mom and grandmother make up their minds, they're like rabid wild animals going in for the kill. Okay, maybe I exaggerate a little, but we're skating kinda close to what happens in real life.

A commotion over by the Christmas tree pulls my attention. A few of the hotel's employees stand nearby, and the concierge stands at attention next to the tree. The crowd gathered in the lobby begins filling in the empty space around the tree, telling me it's almost time for the ceremony. As if on cue, the elevator doors open across the lobby and Maisey walks out, looking absolutely gorgeous.

"Yeah, I could always go out and get a girlfriend. That's a good point, Etta." A very good one indeed. Maisey turns her head from side to side, trying to find me, so I stand up and wave, catching her attention. She spots me, waving, and begins her journey through the throng to join me. "In fact, do me a favor and tell the Terror Twins to not bother with the blind dates."

"Oh?" Etta's voice does this thing where her tone raises up a notch higher, punctuating the end of her word, like she doesn't believe me.

"Don't 'oh' me, Etta. Tell them I have a date."

"Ugh, Jack. You cut out again. What did you say?"

Etta's talking away, but I can't hear her. I only have eyes for one person at this moment, and she's making her way effortlessly through this mass of guests to sit with me. I keep my gaze steady on Maisey, watching her every turn, each smile and whisper of "excuse me" as she finds her way over and stands in front of me.

"Is that seat taken?" she asks coyly, pointing to the empty spot next to me.

"Saved it for you." Standing, I take her hand and help her sit down. Holding my phone in the air, I point to the screen. "Give me two seconds to wrap this up."

Turning my attention back to the phone, I press my lips to the receiver. "Etta, let them know, okay? I'm going to bring someone with me."

The line is silent, then crackles to life two seconds later. Great. There's a delay.

"Jack, I think you said you're going to bring a side dish with you? That's cool and all, but what about this whole Christmas Eve party thing?"

"Etta, listen." I turn my back to the room, which is growing louder by the second. Like turning my back is going to drown out this noise and help with bad reception. "I. Am. Bringing. A. Date. Okay?"

"Yeah, I think you said—" And the line goes dead.

Staring at the phone in my hand, I weigh the option of calling her back when a hand grabs my arm, giving me a gentle tug. Maisey grins up at me and points to her watch.

"It's time."

As she says the words, the giant thirty-foot-tall tree comes to life, its light illuminating her face. The sight is breathtaking, and it feels like we're smack-dab in the middle of a Christmas card. No, we *are* a Christmas card––a Hallmark card at that–– and I want to hold the memory of watching the tree sparkle and twinkle forever and always...but it isn't the tree which has my attention, it's Maisey.

The joyful excitement that floods her features gives me a thrill straight to my very core. Her face glows with excitement as she claps and ooohhs and ahhs. She even shares her appreciation with the other hotel guests who sit nearby, all of them murmuring how beautiful and breathtaking the scene is, while I'm over here watching this woman and thinking the exact same thing.

With the tree officially lit, the crowd begins dispersing, with many of our seatmates saying their goodbyes as they head off to dinner reservations or back to their rooms. I'm about to suggest we think about dinner ourselves when suddenly the small crowd around us parts and Eileen appears like the Ghost of Christmas Present.

"Well, there you are. The couple of the hour." She grabs a chair and slides it next to us to take a seat. "What an adventure it's been having you stay here."

"I take it you spoke to Kelly?" Maisey asks.

Eileen nods. "She explained everything, including how you jumped in right away, Jack, and helped Luke out. Very lucky to have a first responder in the room."

"He's a fireman." If I'm not mistaken, that's pride I hear in Maisey's tone. She waves her left hand in the air. "So was his dad, so it's in his genes."

Eileen must have been watching Maisey's hand because she does a double take before indicating to it.

"I want to ask you a question, Maisey, I just hope it's not

considered rude." Eileen looks pointedly at my fake-fiancée and I stifle a laugh.

Cocking her head to one side, most likely in anticipation of this moment, Maisey holds up her left hand and uses her right to point to it. "Were you going to ask why there's no ring?"

Eileen's eyes bounce back and forth between the two of us. "Yes, but as I started to ask I realized it's another personal question we don't need to know the answer to, so why say anything."

"Come on, Eileen." Maisey leans forward and pats her knee. "I'm sorry for how I reacted. You were doing your job—and it's okay to ask about the ring."

Leaning forward, I take Maisey's hand and hold it tightly in mine. "The ring is a family heirloom; it belonged to my grandmother." Thank goodness we talked about this before we got here. It's the one story I'm prepared for. "It's being sized now so we'll have it for Christmas."

"Ahh." Eileen sits back, mollified for the time being. "Okay, good. My first thought was that you're not really engaged, but how crazy is that? After everything you two have been through since you got here, if you weren't already engaged I'm pretty sure you would be by now."

"How do you know what we've been through since we arrived?" Maisey's brow furrows and a bead of sweat forms at her hairline.

"You fell out of the car when you got here, I heard you fell out of the sleigh, and of course there's the incident with Luke." Eileen's vibe ranges from pity to humor, and it gives me life. Standing, she pats Maisey's shoulder. "Stay prone tonight, we want to say goodbye to you in one piece tomorrow."

As Eileen walks away, Maisey turns to me and wags a

finger. "You could have chimed in and let her know you were the one who had a reaction to their jam."

Fighting my laughter, I lean back against the couch and stretch my arms behind me when I feel something graze my fingertips. Turning around to see what it is, I find one of the Mistletoe's famous snow globes. Stretching a little further, my fingers wrap around the tiny globe and I pull it my way and start shaking it. I'm immediately mesmerized by the snow floating around the circular orb.

"Have you checked in with anyone back home yet?"

"You mean since we've been here?" Maisey shakes her head. "I barely get reception. Honestly, I think if anything was wrong someone would have called. Both Dubs and Dylan know we're here. You would think if an issue came up, someone would at least call the hotel to tell one of us."

Still hypnotized, I turn the globe once more. "True."

"Plus, we're back tomorrow." Maisey nudges me in the ribs. "What's with the sudden interest in the snow globe?"

"This is one of the Mistletoe's holiday snow globes I was telling you about. My mom and grandmother both order their special Christmas edition every year." I lean in and put my lips close to her ear, and am rewarded when I get a whiff of watermelon again. "We've got a lot of snow globes."

"I love them. Hand it over." Laughing, Maisey holds out her hand for the globe and I comply. She grasps the object with both hands, turning and twisting it in every direction, a giddy expression revealing itself on her features.

Using the pointy end of my elbow, I poke her side. "You're a fan?"

"I had a few of these when I was little." She turns the globe upside down on the tiny village inside, starting a small blizzard inside its spherical ecosystem.

"Good evening." A server appears in front of us with two giant hot drinks on a silver tray, which must be hot chocolate judging by the amount of whipped cream piled on top. "Compliments of the house. I was told to extend a special thank you to you, sir. Everyone's talking in the back about the way you helped Luke today."

"It's just what I do." Am I blushing? Probably, or this fire has been stoked and I wasn't aware. The server places the drinks in front of us and leaves, already on to the next guests.

"You're so humble," she teases before taking a swig of her drink. "We should take the time to look around. Want to check out the conservatory?"

I grab my hot chocolate and stand. "Lead the way."

Leaping to her feet, Maisey grabs her mug and blazes a trail across the lobby, down a hall, and into the neighboring wing which houses the Mistletoe Lodge's conservatory.

"We can go at our own pace," she calls out over her shoulder as we cross the entryway, "so any time we want to duck out and head back to the room, we can."

The conservatory is one of the grandest of spaces I've ever set foot in. Tall arched windows look out on a terraced butterfly garden and sculpted shrubs, and it's filled with exotic plants from all parts of the globe. It's also completely decorated for Christmas, keeping us in the spirit with each step.

"This is the room where my grandmother was married." Maisey turns to me with her hands clasped in front of her. "I've seen the photos. It was beautiful."

"Now it makes sense."

Maisey cocks her head to one side. "What does?"

"Your wanting to come here. It makes sense—your grandmother was married here, your mom brought you every year. It's in your DNA."

"I never thought of it like that." She slides her hand into her purse, pulling out an envelope. She holds out the envelope, urging me to take it. "Part of my need to be here was finding this, too."

I hold it in the air. "Should I open it?"

She nods, and I peel back the top layer and slide an invitation out of the envelope. Only it's not just any invitation. It's an invitation from the Mistletoe Lodge to a special ceremony.

Confused, I search Maisey's eyes for an answer. "What is this?"

"It's an invitation my mom received for some reason a few years before she passed away, to a special ceremony in the art gallery to 'Recognize Unsung Heroes.'"

"Do you know why she was invited?"

Maisey shrugged. "Not a clue. I found a record of the event, and it was a big one. The President of the United States was there. I've found folks who attended the event and spoke to them, including some people who worked for the lodge at that time, but no one recognized my mom's name when I told them nor did they understand why she would have been invited."

Tapping my hand with the invitation, which is made from excellent card stock, I watch her face. "It's an event usually reserved for patrons?"

"Exactly. Patrons and special guests of the Mistletoe Lodge" She takes the invitation and envelope out of my grasp and puts it back into her purse. "So that's why I'm here. I'm hoping when we go on that tour tomorrow I'll see something that sparks a memory for me, but if not, I'm going to abide by my new motto."

"What's that?"

"Let it go," she sings as she holds her arms out wide, spinning in a circle.

Caught up in her energy and the moment, I reach out and pull her to me—and she doesn't protest. Something holiday-like plays around us, bless Michael Bublé's heart, but we're in a world of our own. Incredibly, given the crowds here this weekend, we're also completely alone in the magical conservatory...

Maisey presses her body close to mine, and we quickly go from swing dancing to slow dancing. Her body is tight against me, to the point I feel her breath as her chest rises and falls in sync with mine. We're so close I feel the reverberation of her heart slamming inside her body against my chest.

The music stops and the lights in the room fade, and a last call announcement crackles over the intercom letting us know the conservatory is closing for viewing in a few moments. At least I know why we're alone now.

Stepping back, I look down at Maisey to find her focused on something above my head. Glancing up, I'm in no way surprised when I find a giant ball of mistletoe hanging over us.

Maisey's eyes gleam. "Mistletoe."

"It is," I acknowledge. "The symbol of love at Christmas."

"It's actually a...." She stops and closes her eyes. When she finally opens them, they're different. Softer somehow. "Who cares about the history of mistletoe, Jack. I don't."

"I was never any good at retaining history lessons."

"Shhh." She lifts a hand to my lips, her finger stroking the bottom one. My breath hitches, her touch sending a sensation through me equivalent to the tree lighting earlier. I'm alight, alright.

Locking eyes, I inch closer to her and tip her face to mine and smile. "You remind me of that snow globe I was playing with earlier," I whisper.

"Oh?" Maisey dips her chin as she wraps her arms around my neck. "How's that?"

"Well, when you let it sit and be still, it's placid and peaceful. It's what you expect in a snow globe. It's not until you grab it and shake it up that you see its true beauty." I thread my arms around her waist and my grip pulls her in tighter, my heart pounding away.

I didn't think we'd get to this. Not when we left town yesterday, that's for sure. If anyone had said this would be the outcome of a quick trip away with Maisey Montgomery, I would have laughed in their face. It's the outcome I've wanted and wished for, but now it's here and happening. It's happening in my arms. The woman I've been pining for is close enough I can skim my lips across hers, over to her cheek, then down her neck.

Could it be that we're caught up in the moment? Of course. Should I maybe back away and make sure she's thinking clearly? Probably, but her lips are so close to mine.

My finger comes underneath her chin and I tilt it upwards, allowing my mouth to press down and slant across hers. Just a taste before I pull away.

No harm can come from this...can it?

CHAPTER 15

Maisey

I kissed Jack McCoy.

When his lips touched mine, skimming them softly and sweetly, it was like being hit with a wattage of electricity that's measured to infinity. His touch was featherlight on my skin—I can still feel his fingertips dancing along my spine as he pulled me in close to his chest.

Looking at myself in the bathroom mirror, I must admit I'm having a hard time seeing what attracted him. My hair is a mess, I've got toothpaste on my chin, and my mascara is smudged, but every inch of me, from the inside out, tingles. Literally tingling and not from minty fresh breath, even though I'm tempted to take my newly brushed teeth for a spin on Jack's lips.

We'd still be down there, I bet, if we hadn't been kicked out by the security guard.

In my mind, we'd come back to the room and maybe kiss a little more—me having to explain and remind him we're really not engaged nor are we even thinking of marriage, so we need to take a moment.

Am I anxious because we're sharing a bed? More than I

have ever been. Opening the bathroom door, the sight greeting me lets me know I needn't have worried. Jack's in bed already with the table lamp extinguished for the night on his side, and the wall of pillows is stacked back into the perfect border.

I incline my head toward the pillows. "You put them back."

"Of course I did." His silhouette appears as he sits up on his side of the border and runs his fingers through his hair. "I hope that's okay?"

"It's fine." My shoulders instantly relax, even though my tummy tightens a little in disappointment. Did I like kissing him? Did I ever. But it's a lot of feelings rising to the surface at once, and considering I've been kinda-sorta mad at him for a few months, I'd be ridiculous if I didn't admit I was confused by my reaction.

Yet, I'm also *not* totally confused by it. Because it's Jack, and no matter what, I come back to the fact I've had a crush on this man for a very long time. He's maddening, and he's charming. He's frustrating, but he's also hilarious. He's all strength, but he's as gentle as a butterfly.

Sliding under the sheets, I snuggle in and turn toward the pillow wall. "Actually, can we take a few of those down so I can see you?"

Jack chuckles and removes the pillows for the big reveal. His teeth practically sparkle when he smiles, his grin lighting up even the most dimly lit room. "This better?"

"A little. Maybe a few more?"

"Sure." He takes a few more away, tossing them to the floor, before turning back to face me. "I think we should stop there."

"Are you sure?" In an instant, I regret these words coming from my mouth. Where is nervous Maisey from mere moments ago? She's been replaced by insane-hormones-raging Maisey, thank you, and she wants things she shouldn't.

This Maisey is like a wild creature let loose in the animal kingdom.

"I'm sure." He chuckles, while I stew in my embarrassment soup for one. Of course I'm pushing it too far. What am I thinking? I'm contemplating an excuse so I can go make my bed on the couch when I feel the brush of something against my arm. A second later, Jack's fingers reach out and stroke the back of my hand. "Can we hold hands?"

"I'd like that." His touch on my skin sends a shiver reverberating through me. I wrap his hand in mine.

Jack strokes my hand gently, tracing tiny lines across the back of it with his fingertips, each touch sending a sensation through me that rivals the other. It's hot, and it's cold, and it leaves my skin on fire.

"Hey, Maisey," he says after he clears his throat. "There's this thing I need to do this week and well, I was wondering if you'd like to come with me to my family's Christmas party?"

My ears perk up as a tiny thrill courses through my chest. "Oh?"

He shifts his position. "Is that weird?"

"No. Well, a little." How do I say it's Christmas, we just kissed, and I'm still wrapping my head around the fact I have issues because I didn't like you and now I'm ready to admit I did the whole time? "You sure you want to bring me around your family?"

Jack chuckles and squeezes my hand. "Positive. You'll have a blast, and they'll love you."

"I guess I can—"

"Also, I did come here and pretend to be your fiancé."

Ah. Tit for tat. "What time do I need to be there?"

His infectious laugh fills the room as he pulls his hand from mine and in turn wraps mine in his. "We'll figure it out. I'm glad you said yes."

"Blackmail. Works a treat." I'm joking, because I would

have said yes anyway. Especially if it meant another kiss. That last one was too fleeting.

Lying there in the darkness, the smile draped across my face rivals a clown's. I'm a woman content. I kissed him and he kissed me, and it was easily the best kiss I've ever had. Or gotten for that matter. My free hand flies to my lips, the sensation of Jack's still imprinted on them.

Wondering how it is we made it to here, I feel my eyes growing heavy. Giving up, I let myself succumb to sleep, the sound of Jack's gentle snoring the last thing I hear and the touch of his hand wrapped around mine the last thing I feel for the night.

* * *

"What do you mean there's no art exhibition today, either?"

The serene memory of last night fades away as I deal with my nemesis, Eileen. Checkout wasn't until eleven this morning, but since we had wanted to sneak in our tours before we leave and head back to Lake Lorelei, we'd packed up and gone to the lobby early.

"It's closed to visitors. There was a mishap with one of the Christmas trees. It fell over in the middle of the night, so the team is in there now cleaning up and replacing it." She clasps her hands on the countertop. "I'm so sorry."

"That includes the snow globes, too?" Jack's voice goes up an octave, and it catches the attention of a security guard stationed in the lobby. He's across the room and standing by us at the reception desk in a flash.

"It does. I'm sorry." Eileen gives us one of her half-smiles, the kind that's void of any sincerity. I feel like she wants to get rid of us.

"Oh." My head hangs low as I tap the countertop. Thinking about the photo and invitation stashed in my purse hanging on my shoulder, I'm hit with a pang of sadness. "Well, I guess that's it, then."

"No. No, it isn't." Jack steps up to the counter and leans in. "It's part of our package, Eileen. You said we'd get to see the art gallery and the snow globes today. I don't think it's a good look for you or the Mistletoe Lodge if the winners of your romantic getaway do not get all of the prizes they were promised, do you?"

While Jack's standing on his soapbox, my spidey senses tingle to life. Something about karma resonates in my mind. I put my hand on Jack's forearm to stop him but, as my eyes find Eileen's, I realize it's too late.

"Well, Jack, I don't think it would be a good look for the residents of Lake Lorelei to know that the captain of their fire department and the owner of the favorite local cafe were here, staying at our hotel for free, and lying to us about being engaged." She stands back and crosses her arms, clearly the victor.

Crap.

I nudge Jack out of the way. "I can explain…"

Eileen shakes her head. "Oh, there's no need. I know what you did." She points her finger at me, then at Jack, then back to me again. "I know what both of you did."

"Sounds like a movie." Jack picks the wrong time to throw down a joke. "I know what you did…last Christmas."

"Not funny," Eileen and I snap in unison.

"Geez." Jack holds up his hands feigning surrender.

"It was my idea, Eileen. I could have told you and I didn't, and I'm sorry." I want to crawl over this counter and grovel at this woman's feet. I'm horrified, and not only for being busted.

"I have every right to charge you for your full stay and all of the activities you enjoyed, you know. It's in the fine print."

We bob our heads up and down, like a couple of underage kids being put in their place.

"But," she hisses as she puts both hands on the desk and grips it. "I'm not."

"You have very right...wait." A rush of cold hits my veins and my jaw goes slack. "What?"

"Jack gave one of our employees first aid yesterday when he didn't have to. And"—she turns to me—"our conversation about our 'get to know you' questions has changed the way we're going to operate when we work with newly engaged couples. We've been a factory for so long, we forgot to put the personal back into our efforts. That's a lesson I don't think we would have gotten if you hadn't have come."

"That's so kind of you." It's like a weight, one that was suddenly dropped on my head, is gone now and the pressure is relieved. But only for a second.

"That's not really kind, it's luck on your part. And, you do need to pay the piper, it's just not how you think." She stands stick straight again and peers at me through squinted eyes. "I need something in return, and I need it on January first."

"Okay." My gaze rests on Jack, whose eyes are wide with encouragement. I turn my focus back to Eileen. If I'm going to have to take one for the team, then I will. "What is it?"

"I need an order of forty pumpkin pies delivered. I Googled you, Maisey Montgomery, and you're quite the baker." Eileen grins as she visibly relaxes. "I think if you provide our kitchen staff working on New Year's Day with their own homemade pie to take home as a present from the Mistletoe Lodge, we can call it even...until the next time I deem appropriate to cash in a favor, that is."

"Done." I shove my hand across the desk and pump Eileen's fiercely.

"I have to ask," Jack interrupts. "How did you find out?"

"Maisey was recognized in the conservatory last night."

Eileen nods at the security guard. "Apparently you and John were matched on a dating app a few weeks ago."

"Ohhh." That thing. I knew I never should have joined that app.

"Anyway, that all went better than expected." Eileen waves a hand in the air and the man she calls John, aka the traitorous security guard who told on me, appears beside Jack. "John, please take these two to meet Theo. They have a final tour of the art gallery to get through before they leave."

My eyes find Eileen's and she's smiling at us. "I am not condoning your actions, but I am glad we found a way for all of us to walk away happy." She nods her head in Jack's direction. "Also, if the two of you really aren't a couple, I need to ask what is wrong with you? You're perfect for each other."

With that, Eileen steps away from the desk and throws one last wave our way before disappearing behind a wall. Spinning to face Jack, I clap my hands together.

"All right, let's do this tour and get out of here." I hold one hand in the air, waiting for him to do the same.

Jack looks at my hand and, shaking his head, raises his and smacks them together for a cracking high five.

"Let's do this."

CHAPTER 16

Maisey

Theo made sure we walked the snow globe exhibit first, and Jack was thrilled to get a private showing. He snapped photos for his family, picked out two special edition snow globes for his mom and grandmother—ones not even released to the public yet—and even put a few snow globes aside to take home, I think for himself.

A tidbit I learned about Jack McCoy today is that he loves giving gifts. He's like a kid in a candy store when he's picking things out for others and it's the cutest thing to witness. Like the way he wanted Theo to bring me to the art gallery as soon as we were done so I could finally do what I wanted, too.

Finally, we're here. I take a deep breath, exhaling slowly as I clutch the photo I brought with me close to my chest. Closing my eyes, I slip away for a moment to a time when life felt easy, every day was about waking up and playing as hard as I could, and when I got hurt or skinned my knee, my mom was there to fix it.

The room smelled of old—if that can even be a smell—a combined scent of old wood, musk, and a hint of lemon, probably from the cleaners. When I open my eyes, Jack's sparkling blue eyes greet me.

"Happy?" The lazy half-smile draped on his lips as he watches me sends a shiver to my very core.

"So happy." Holding up the photograph, I cast my eyes around the giant room. "This was taken in here; I just need to figure out where."

"Unless they've rearranged things, we should be able to find the art piece you were standing in front of." Jack's eyes flick from the photo to the walls surrounding us. We both turn around in circles, inspecting the room, but in the end, we're both stumped.

"I don't see it." A rock slams into my stomach. No, scratch that, it's a rock slide. Did I really obsess all this time over nothing?

"Let's keep looking for that picture." Jack reaches out and grabs my arm, squeezing it. "It's gotta be here."

The realization that my efforts might not be rewarded today hits home. "I can't believe it. I've waited all this time to come here and resurrect some long forgotten memory and for what? It's gone." I hold the photo in the air. "Like my mom."

"Hey, Maisey." Jack pulls me in close when tears spring to my eyes. I'm stunned into submission and praying I can pull it together when Theo pipes in.

"Maybe I can be of help." He'd been hanging back, letting us do our thing under his watchful eye, but now he stands with us. He holds his hand out. "May I see the photo?"

I pass it to him and watch as he studies it. Theo turns around, his eyes scanning the room. When his eyes land on something he thinks is of use to our mystery, he inclines his head toward the opposite end of the room.

"There." I follow his gaze to the far corner. "That's where this photo was originally taken, but the wallpaper has been replaced since then and"—he points to the framed work of art in the background of the photograph—"that particular piece is no longer out on the floor for public viewing. But I know where it is. Come with me."

Jack and I exchange glances, with Jack shrugging his shoulders. "What's the harm?"

Figuring he's right, we plod behind Theo across the great room, exiting the other side and following him down a side hallway. In a matter of moments we exit the wing and find ourselves in another section of the house.

Theo continues on his mission, marching ahead of us. I quicken my pace so I can walk next to him. "We're not near the gallery any longer, are we?"

"No, Dorothy, we're not." Theo comes to a stop outside of a room, a plaque on the wall announcing it as the Music Room. He taps on the door. "But we are close to Oz."

He opens the door, showing us into a room filled with nothing but artwork. I recognize a Monet in the corner, a Renoir hanging across the room, and one of Botticelli's most famous works, *Adoration of the Magi*, is front and center on display—the one from my photograph.

"So, it's here?" My eyes bounce back and forth from my photo to the art around us. "Whenever I looked up this painting by Botticelli, everything says it's housed at the National Gallery of Art."

"In Washington D.C.?" Jack asks.

Theo nods. "It is. We happen to have it here for a special exhibition we'll be hosting in January for the new year."

Eyeing Theo, the feeling of recognition washes over me like a small wave hitting the shore, and goosebumps flicker across my flesh. "You've worked here a long time, haven't you?"

He gives a slight bow of his head and grins at me. "I have."

"Have you always been a butler here?" Sliding the envelope out of my purse, I pull out the invitation my mother received, keeping it clutched tightly in my grasp for now.

"No, I've had several positions with the lodge over the years." His eyes twinkle. "My father worked here, as did his father. They were both butlers and then concierges, but we all started in security for the art gallery. It's a rite of passage."

"Your grandfather worked here?" Jack crosses his arms in front of his chest. "That's cool you walked in his footsteps."

"Jack did the same. His dad was a fireman, too. In New York City." Is that pride in my voice? Yep. Sure is.

Theo smiles at Jack. "I wanted to be a fireman, but I was scared of fire."

Jack laughs. "Then you chose your profession wisely."

Chuckling, Theo's eyes wander back to the photo in his hands. "You know, I had a feeling when I saw you that I knew who you were, Maisey."

Something in his voice sends another chill across my body, leaving even more goosebumps in its wake. "What do you mean?"

"I took this picture of you, your sister, and your mom." He smiles as he hands it back to me. "Your mother was a regular every year. She came here for Christmas because it's what her mother taught her to do, but I'm sure you know about all of that, right?"

Not quite sure I understand, I shake my head. "About all of what?"

"Your grandmother used to work here. In fact"—he looks at both Jack and I, his eyes dancing—"she was an integral part of helping the United States government during World War II."

My jaw drops and my hand reaches for Jack's automatically, but luckily he's already sliding an arm around my waist, as if he was anticipating holding me up. "What?"

"Your grandmother worked here during the winter of

1942. That was the year the director for the National Gallery of Art reached out and asked if the Mistletoe Lodge would help hide some of their pieces." His brow furrows as he takes his side trip down memory lane, bringing us with him. "There was information that Hitler wanted to come to America and seize art here, too, as was being done in Europe, so they needed to put a plan in place to keep our nation's works safe."

My jaw hurts from unhinging. "My grandmother helped?"

Theo laughs. "When the art arrived, literally under the cloak of night, we stored it here, in the music room. No one ever knew it was here, and we were open to the public at that time. Your grandmother and my grandfather were stationed together outside of the room to help direct tourists and visitors away. Even though the door was locked and we had security staff, they kept two employees on 'guard' twenty-four hours a day until the threat was over."

"So Maisey's grandmother has had a hand in helping to save famous pieces of art, kinda like the monument men in the movies?" Jack's face is incredulous, a true mirror of my insides at this precise moment.

"That's exactly right." Theo turns to me and points to the wall behind me. "In fact, there's a plaque over there with her name on it."

Spinning on my heel, I take a few long strides until I'm standing in front of the plaque, scanning the names. Seeing my grandmother's there, I rub my finger across it and smile.

I turn around, my eyes finding Jack's. "My grandmother. Can you believe this?"

He points to the envelope in my other hand. "Don't forget to ask about the invitation, too."

"What invitation?" Theo asks.

I hand him the envelope. He slides the invitation out, and upon seeing it, his expression softens even more.

"I remember this event. Both your grandmother and my grandfather were honored that night for their work. The President of the United States came for a special dinner and handed out plaques to their surviving family members. We never heard from your mom, but we figured she would get in touch some day. Only she never did."

Tears sting at the back of my eyes. "She was spiraling into dementia and Alzheimer's when the invite was sent. We never knew about it. We never knew about any of this."

The tears flowing now, I use my sleeve to wipe my wet cheeks when Jack stops me and shoves a tissue in my hands. I whisper "thank you" and turn around, taking a moment to dab my cheeks and gather myself. It's not often you find out the amazing village you hail from, in this case mine is my family, is made up of superheroes who had a hand in history. It's a little overwhelming.

"Hey." Two arms slide around my waist from behind, Jack pulling me in close to his chest and holding me tight. "How are you doing with processing all of this information?"

"I'm...processing." I lean my head back so it rests on his shoulder and angle my face so we're cheek to cheek. I've never been more grateful to have someone with me than I am right now. Bonus that he's holding me, too. He is safety.

Theo looks at his watch. "I hate to do this, but I know you want to get on the road."

Jack and I untangle ourselves and I walk up to Theo and wrap my arms around him, not even able to stop myself.

"Thank you for today. I can't believe it's you who was able to help me figure out this little mystery."

"I'm glad it happened. It's like we were supposed to meet, Maisey." He steps back and holds his hand out to shake Jack's. "Before you go, I'll get the staff to wrap up your grandmother's plaque, the one your mother was going to accept for her, and you can take it home with you."

"Thanks again," Jack says as we follow Theo and exit the room. "This has been a great trip."

"You won't have any reason to not come back now," Theo added. "Because the Mistletoe gifted all the descendants of their Art Gallery Protection Team lifetime passes to the Estate and all exhibits."

"Well, looks like you won't get rid of me now," I tease with a wink.

"I hope we see you again very soon." Theo's eyes are lit up with life and joy as he looks back and forth at us, indicating that he's referring to us both.

With a dip of his head, he's gone. Leaving us alone and me in his wake to revel in the amazingness that is my family.

* * *

"Honestly, I can't believe that just happened." Jack grips the wheel, concentrating on the winding mountain road. He's been in a state of shock since we left. I'm not sure if he's in shock for me or the price he had to pay for those snow globes.

"It was a Christmas miracle, I guess." Rounding a corner, the car comes through a clearing and we're on a stretch of road with more population. We'd taken back roads to go home, stretching out the getaway feel a little longer.

When I see the sign telling us we're five miles outside of Lake Lorelei, I'm not surprised to hear my phone begin beeping, signaling we're back in full cell reception once again.

"Well, that break was nice while it lasted," Jack says as his phone starts beeping, too.

Grabbing my phone, messages flash to life from everyone. Ari, who handles the cafe's social media, has sent me a lot of texts; Craig sent our weekly food order so I know what to expect; and Dylan takes the cake clocking in with thirty-two missed texts.

Tapping the app and reading Dylan's texts, the urge to hurl my Sunday breakfast all over Jack's truck is strong.

"Oh no." I swallow and turn in my seat to face Jack. "It's all over social media. The marketing team tagged us and it's everywhere that we were there."

Jack simply shrugs, not understanding. "We'll deal with it when we get home."

"You're not hearing me." I shake the phone in the air. "The Mistletoe Lodge posted pics of their engaged winners. Look." I point to the photos on my phone. "See these pics, the ones with lots of comments? Those are photos of us and those comments are locals in Lake Lorelei saying congrats."

"Maisey, it's fine." Jack reaches over and pats my leg. "We'll explain when we see people, okay? No need to worry at all."

"Jack, you don't get it. There are close to one thousand comments on this photo. North Carolina is not a large state, and Lake Lorelei is not that big of a town. I'm willing to bet money your family has seen this."

Judging by the way the color fades from his cheeks, he finally understands. Bless his heart. He hands me his phone.

"My passcode is 010199. Can you tell me how many texts or missed calls I've gotten?"

"You should rethink that code for better security." My attempt at joking fails when I get no response. I plug the code in and let out a whistle. "Wow. Only ten missed calls, but there are texts from someone named Etta and looks like you have a few from your mom as well."

"Okay. I can handle this." Slowing the car, Jack turns right off the highway and pulls onto Main Street, pointing the car in the direction of the firehouse where I left my car parked a few days prior.

"It's your mom, Jack, she'll be confused, but all of that can be straightened out when you talk to her and explain."

"You don't know my family or my situation, Maisey." Pulling the car over, Jack maneuvers expertly into a parking space in front of the firehouse. He puts the car in park and stares straight ahead. "I'm not only dealing with my mom."

Where did the guy go who had his arms wrapped around me a few hours earlier? That guy was open to letting me in so I could learn more about his family and his mom. That guy asked me to help pick out a snow globe for his grandmother, and he's the same guy who finally let me in and shared about his loss.

"Hey." I put my hand on his arm. "I feel like this is all because of me. What can I do?"

"If you feel like that, it's because it is. It does all come back to you." He shakes his head, his eyes looking out beyond the windshield, scanning the area as if he expected someone or something to appear. "Thanks for offering, but there's nothing you can do."

While I continue my quiet battle to keep the day's food down, Jack suddenly sits up straight in his seat. Quick as a flash, he turns off the engine and climbs out, leaving me in the dust.

Ever the gentleman, he makes sure to open the trunk, pull my bags out, and place them on the curb before he starts to go. I fight the urge to roll my eyes and scream "I knew it!"

"Sorry, Maisey, but I need to run." He grabs me and gives me a half-hearted hug. "I'll call you later this week about the party, okay?"

"Yeah, sounds good." I barely mumble my response and he's gone, disappearing around the corner and out of sight. Sighing, I pick up my bags and head to the back parking lot of the firehouse to get my car.

I manage to get in my car quickly, throwing it into reverse while visions of anything sugar dances in my head. I'm beginning to get giddy about picking up some takeout and treating myself to a piece of cake when I pull out of the lot and onto Main Street.

Sitting at a stoplight one block away—still trying to decide if I want chocolate cake or vanilla—I look to my left and see a couple embracing. As it sinks in one half of said couple is Jack, my heart does a deep dive, sinking into my stomach and releasing another wave of nausea through my being.

When he pulls away, I realize I recognize the other person from a few months ago. She's gorgeous. She's smiling at him and holding a snow globe in her free hand, shaking it as she kisses his cheek. The stunning redhead throws her thick mane back over her shoulder, then loops her arm through his as they turn and make their way down the street.

Well. Looks like I'm not the only one into being fake these days.

CHAPTER 17

Jack

"So, when do I get to meet this fiancée of yours?" Making our way down Main Street and heading to the grocery store, Etta gives me her best side-eye while she shakes her snow globe. "And I'd love to know how your date, the one who's coming to the party, is going to take the news. Hopefully as well as your mom and grandmom did."

"They don't even have social media, how do they know about the Mistletoe Lodge?" For two women who claim to not know how to use technology, I feel duped.

"Did you really think this town is so small and off the beaten path you'd get away with going off and playing house for a few days?" Etta chuckles. "You're such an amateur at handling our mother. She found out through a friend of hers in town this morning. She called to congratulate Mom on the new addition to the family. Turns out Maisey is well-liked. Can't wait to meet her."

"But I'm not engaged, Etta." Rolling my eyes, I stop in my tracks.

"I know this and you know this, but the Terror Twins

don't. And"—she taps my arm knowingly—"It's best if they don't know. Otherwise, more blind dates for you."

Well, there's a bright side. "Do you think this will stop them from setting me up on any more dates, at least for the season?"

"I mean, invitations have already gone out for the party. And, to be fair, your connection was terrible when we talked and I thought you were joking, so I didn't tell them you were bringing someone."

"You would think that there won't be any surprises, like blind dates on Christmas Eve, right?"

Etta shrugs and holds up her hand, showing me her fingers are crossed.

"Great." I exhale so loudly and with such force Etta's hair blows in its wake.

"Dude. Why are you being so...dramatic?"

"Because." I shove my hands in my jacket pockets. "I kind of messed up with this one, Etta. She's special and I actually want to try this time. With Maisey."

Etta squints and crosses her arms, hugging herself. "What do you mean you messed up and 'try this time?'"

"Let's just say I had a chance with Maisey but I—I asked her out and Kara died. Liam needed us, and so did the kids. I put everything, including her, on the backburner."

"As you should have." Of course my twin is going to take my side.

"But, I never told her why I disappeared. This trip came about and I was lucky enough to get another chance to try again."

"Ah, now I see." Clasping her hands in front of her, she eyes me and nods her head slowly. "So you ghosted her. Nice. I get why you're counting your lucky stars she gave you another shot, 'cause I wouldn't have."

"I didn't ghost her." Okay, maybe by definition I did, but

it's also a small town so it's not like I disappeared completely. "I chose to avoid the topic of our date for a period of time, and in turn it made her mad. Not that I can blame her. I didn't communicate with her what was going on so she didn't know. So that's why I needed the second chance, Etta. I wanted to make it right because she's worth it."

"Whoa." Etta's eyes grow wide as she takes two steps back to look at me. She drags her eyes from the top of my head to the bottom of my feet and back again. "I think you're falling in…"

"Zip it." I hold my hand in the air and act like I'm catching her words. "I'll decide when and where those words are used."

Etta swats at me, and I manage to sidestep her swing but also to drop my phone at the same time. Groaning, I pick it up and find the screen smashed. "Great."

"Oh, man, Jack." Etta stands on her tiptoes and peers over my shoulder. "Crap. That doesn't look like it's going to work anytime soon."

"No, it doesn't." Making a face, I slide it in my pocket. "I can get a new phone when I'm out later this week. I'm working the next few days in a row at the station, so I don't need my phone. I can use the house line."

"I can't decide if your life is interesting or complicated," Etta says with a laugh. "What I do know is if you don't get all of this straightened out, and fast, the Christmas Eve party is going to be soooo interesting."

* * *

Maisey

Knocking on Dylan's door, I look around but don't see her car in the driveway. Dylan and Dubs live right off Main Street, not too far from the firehouse. Dubs owns the local garage, which is another block in the opposite direction, so it's handy they live in the center of their own little world. At least it's good for me today for a quick pit stop to unload on my best friend on the way home.

Thinking she's probably not here, I start walking back to my car. I'm halfway down the sidewalk when the front door opens behind me.

"Hey," Dylan calls out. "Get back here."

I all but skip up the steps and hug my friend, tears welling as I do. Dylan sees my upset, ushering me inside and into the kitchen for a hot cup of tea immediately.

"Oh, wow. Holy all the things." It's the only response she can muster after I fill her in on everything, right up to seeing Jack hugging the mystery woman before I came over. "So you just got back into town?"

"Not even gone home yet. I'm confused and reeling, and questioning everything." Pulling out a chair at her kitchen table, I slide into the seat. "I left here promising myself I could play nice and put my crush and irritation with that man behind me, and I come back wanting more from him."

"That's progress, right?" Dylan slides a steaming mug of peppermint tea in front of me.

"Until I see him hugging all over some woman." I hold the mug between my hands, letting the warmth seep into my icy fingers. "After everything we went through this weekend, I thought we were finally on the same page, or at least we were in the same chapter."

Seeing Dylan's phone on the table in front of me, I point to it. "May I?"

"Sure." She walks over, punches in her code to unlock it, and hands it back to me. At which time, I promptly dial Jack's number and luckily I'm sent to his voicemail. From here, it's a few clicks of some buttons, until I enter his passcode—yes, I memorized it—and voilà …I'm able to re-record his outgoing message.

I wait for the beep to ding in my ear before I begin. "Hi. This is Jack McCoy's answering service. He's not able to answer because he's very busy right now being a fireman who tells fibs. He wanted me to communicate this to you now so you know, instead of giving you any surprises in the future. Happy holidays and have a great day."

A few more taps and it's done. Triumphantly, I hand the phone back to Dylan.

"I hope you feel better now that you have that out of your system." She's quite smug this one.

"I feel great." I'm lying. I know I just pushed it too far and I want to save face.

"Look here, my little conclusion jumper." Dylan takes a sip from her mug, then places it down on the counter in front of her. "You have no idea who that woman is; you're only guessing. You were moaning a moment ago about how Jack hadn't really talked to you about any of this with you until now."

"Yeah, so?"

"Well," Dylan says with a chuckle, "don't assume anything. Next time you see him, ask him about her. You agreed to go to his family party as his date to help him out, right?"

"Well, yeah." I have a feeling I know where this is going.

"So ask him then. Or if you see him before the party. When is it?"

"It's this Friday."

"Okay, so ask him when you see him. Who knows?" Dylan tosses a hand in the air. "Could be his sister."

"Could be, and if it is I'll eat my ski hat." I wag my finger at Dylan. "It's too convenient if it is his 'sister' and yes, I am using air quotes because we don't know if it is or not."

"I can't argue with you there. I didn't know he had a sibling until now; it's not like he's ever talked about any of this with any of us at the firehouse."

"Who hasn't talked about what?" Dubs' voice booms, echoing off the kitchen walls as he enters the room. Spotting us in our positions, me at the table hunched over my mug and Dylan at the counter like she's my adult supervision, he stops. "Did I interrupt something?"

"Just my sad lack of love life." Using my foot I pull out a chair and tilt my chin in its direction. "Please, join me. It is your house."

Dubs settles in beside me as Dylan's phone goes off in her hand.

"You'd better not forget to change that outgoing message you just recorded, missy," she says as she wags a finger in my direction before walking away, her face buried in her phone.

"Your love life isn't that bad if you're engaged." Dubs winks and nudges me with his elbow. "At least, word on the street has it that you are."

"Small towns, small states." Sighing, I lay my head on my hands on the tabletop. "I guess I can add my small mind to that list."

"Girl, your mind isn't small, but your attitude is." Dubs sits back in his chair, drumming his fingers on the table. "Dylan isn't wrong. Jack's tightlipped about his personal life with the gang at work, but I know one person he isn't so quiet with."

I cock my head to one side. "And who is that?"

Dubs jerks a thumb at his chest. "Moi. I spend a lot of time with him, so we talk."

"You do?" Glancing across the kitchen, I see Dylan is checked out of our convo and madly texting with whoever is on the other end of her phone.

"Uh huh." Dubs nods his head slowly, a funny smile

spreading across his features. "He's very private, and if he took the time to trust you and told you about what he's been through, which it sounds like he has, then he thinks very highly of you, Maisey."

Swallowing, I stare at my hands in my lap. I know Dubs isn't going to tell me something simply for the sake of trying to make me feel better. He's telling me this for a reason.

A feeling of calm washes over me as Dylan marches up to the table and slams her phone on it.

"I take back everything I said about Jack that's nice." She looks at me, her eyes riddled with worry. "That was this girl I know from my yoga class. She wanted to ask me about Jack and what he likes. It seems she's been asked to go to his family's Christmas party this Friday as a set-up."

There is no more nausea to rise from deep within, only pure disappointment. Patting the table with my hands, I stand up and put my jacket on. "I need to go."

Dylan looks at her dad and holds her arms out to her sides. "Is it a man thing?"

"Uh huh." Dubs shakes his head and holds his hands in front of him in mock surrender. "I'm not going to get in the middle of this. I told you what I know."

"I get it." I lean over and give him a hug on my way out the door. Dylan is hot on my heels, asking me to call her if I need to talk later.

"I'll be fine." Am I the one who's fibbing now? One hundred percent, but in this case I need to do it so I can go home and crawl under my comforter and hide. "I'll still go as his date to the party because he came with me to the Mistletoe, but then after that there will be no more pining over Jack McCoy."

"There could be a simple explanation, you know." Dylan calls out as I jog down her sidewalk.

Pivoting, I shrug and give her my best "who knows"

expression. I'm doing my best to act like I'm okay even though I'm hurt. Really hurt and really disappointed. I shove my hands in my pockets, put my head down, and head up the street to where my car's parked.

Making my way up the street, my thoughts wander as I put my feet on autopilot. The whole idea of a relationship with Jack was kinda doomed; at least by my calculations they were. Sifting through the last few days, I can't deny I had fun. That he made me laugh and feel alive, especially when he was close to me or his skin touched mine. Surely something positive can still come out of his whole crazy situation?

My mind still swirls when my body slams into another person, their shoulder cracking into mine as we bounce off one another like pinballs.

"Ow!" My hand flies to my shoulder and I rub it. Turning around, I tap the shoulder of the woman I ran into. "So sorry I didn't see you."

As the redhead lifts her face to mine, a cold tingle works its way through me. I hadn't run into just anyone on the street. I'd managed to slam into Jack's mystery woman.

The stunning creature stands in front of me, rubbing her shoulder as well. When she finally makes eye contact, there's a flicker of surprised recognition and a knowing look spreads across her face.

"Well, well," she says as she looks me up and down. "I was wondering how I could find you."

Dumbfounded, I take a step back. "Huh?"

She smiles and holds out her hand. "I'm Etta, Jack's sister. We need to talk."

CHAPTER 18

Jack

'Twas the night before Christmas and all through the house, all the creatures were stirring. All of them 'cause we're about to have a party. Not that this house is ever silent at the holidays, in fact it's the opposite. And I love it.

Standing at the top of the stairs, my view allows me to see perfectly into the living room and I can make out the foyer and front door beyond. Guests trickle in, the tree lights twinkle, and underneath its branches is a plethora of presents in all shapes and sizes. I'm reveling in holiday wonder and bemusement when someone tugs at my sleeve.

"Uncle Jack, are you going to read the story to me?"

Looking down, my niece, Vivian, grins up at me and her fraternal twin, Levi, holds *The Night Before Christmas* in his wee hands. Tousling his hair, I scoop Vivian into my arms.

"Maybe later, after everyone's left." I give Vivian a squeeze before setting her back down, and at the same time the bedroom door behind me creaks open.

"Thought I heard you out here." Liam claps me on the

back and stands beside me, tossing an arm around my shoulders. "How are you holding up?"

Of course Etta had filled my brother in on my plight with Maisey and our fake engagement. He'd been a star player for our team this week, helping to keep my mom and grandmother busy while I stayed clear of the house. Last thing I wanted was to add more fuel to the fire, so the goal is to get through tonight and then I'll deal with the consequences.

"Good so far." Pulling my phone out of my pocket, I'm disappointed to see the one person I've been hoping to hear from has not texted me. Yet. Or at all this week, actually, except once. She did text Sunday night thanking me for going and promising to be here tonight, but since then it's been radio silent.

And, not that I'm a weirdo stalker, but I did see Craig and he told me Maisey's been busy coming into work earlier than usual to stay on top of her holiday bakery orders. Yeah, guess I'm a little obsessed, but I think it's in a good way.

"You're pretty tense for a man who is allegedly introducing his family to his fiancée tonight," Liam says, his hand flying to his mouth in an effort to push a laugh back in that mug of his. "Sorry, every time I think about how insane this whole thing is, it cracks me up." Proving his point, he snorts.

"Good one." Swiping at his arm, I manage to graze it before he steps out of the way.

"Come on, Daddy." Vivian's little hand threads its way into her father's. "Can we have eggnog now?"

"Of course, my little sugarplum." Watching Liam kiss the top of her head, my heart hitches. I see Kara reflected in so much of these two and I'm sure Liam does as well. It can't be easy.

As if reading my thoughts, he turns to me. "It's been a hard year, but I think Kara would be proud of how we're doing, don't you?"

Smiling, he takes a twin in each hand and the trio head downstairs. Liam stops when he hits the landing and calls out to me at the top of the steps. "You may want to check your voicemail. Not sure what's going on with it, but Mom said she tried to call you and the message is weird."

Stumped, I haven't a clue what he's talking about. "Maybe it's because I only got my new phone today?"

Liam shrugs as the kids push him into the living room. Before I can ask any follow-up questions, the picture of absolute sweetness wrapped as my family disappears out of sight ready to welcome Santa and read stories by the fireside. I'll deal with my voicemail later.

Sighing, I park in the closest chair outside of my grandmother's room and swipe the neatly wrapped gift off the side table beside me. Maisey's present—if she makes it tonight so I can give it to her, that is—sits next to a photo of my grandparents on their wedding day and another photo of my grandfather, who we always called Gramps.

Gramps passed away a long time ago, when I was still in high school. But I know from the stories Gran told me over the years how much he would have loved seeing me grow up, how much I act like he did. Being here in his presence feels big. Like I'm not living up to what he would expect if he was still here.

Picking up the framed photograph, I hold it in my hands. I see the resemblance when I look into his eyes; it's like I see me. "Gramps, in some ways I wish you were here. And in other ways, I know you'd be really disappointed if you knew I'd lied to Mom and Gran and let them think I'm engaged."

Since the photo isn't going to talk back to me, I keep going. "The thing is, I like this woman. Nope. Take it back, I love her." When I hear the words spoken out loud, it gives me a sensation. It's warm and it floods my body, sending a shiver running up and down my spine.

"Gramps, I love her." Holding the gift in my hands, I toss it from one hand to the other, feeling as if a weight is rising off my shoulders. "I cannot believe I'm gonna say this sentence out loud, but I am. I love my fake fiancée."

"Why you little sneak." Behind me, a door slams. My head snaps to the right, where Gran is standing with a hand covering her mouth. She drops it and sets me squarely in her sights, pointing a finger in my direction.

"You little storyteller, you." Shaking her finger, she walks closer to me. "Before I go drop this knowledge on your mom, fess up."

Did my little Gran just say "dropping knowledge?" Indeed. This woman listens to the Beastie Boys. It came after Liam and I made her listen to them on repeat one summer. My family is ridiculously cool.

So, I spilled it all. Everything. From the asking out on a date, to not actually going on one. To the essay and subsequent win, to Maisey asking me to go with her so she could do what she needed to do. By the end of it, Gran has made me get out of my seat so she can sit down and take it all in.

"Oh my goodness, you kids these days make it all very complicated, don't you?" Pretending her hand is a fan, she waves it in front of her face. "Okay, tell you what. I'm going to help you fix this and fast, but do me a favor and listen."

I hold my hands in the air. "I'm all ears."

"Being in a relationship of any kind takes work, but when we're in love, the stakes get so much higher." Reaching out, she takes the photo out of my hands and smiles at Gramps, kissing the glass. "I know Maisey from around town, and I know what a catch she is. Trust me, if she means something to you, don't let her slip past, Jack. Did you know your grandfather and I got engaged after three dates?"

This is news to me. "What? No way."

A knowing smile pulls on her lips and her eyes sparkle

with a wisdom I hope I'm lucky enough to imbibe one day. "Yep. We knew by the third date we wanted to be together. We were married two months later, and from there we figured it out. You know what it comes down to?"

I shake my head. "I think if I knew that I'd be the richest human on the face of the earth."

"True." She laughs. "But the answer is easy. You gotta talk. To each other. Communicate and be open, don't hold things in."

It's almost as if she's been in my pocket the last week and knew how good I'd gotten at keeping things in. I can't deny she's right, though.

"I'm sorry I didn't tell you and Mom the truth about being engaged. At first, I was bringing Maisey because I didn't want any blind dates here, but...things changed when we went away last weekend."

"Don't worry, Etta shut down the blind dates a few nights ago, when she told me what was going on." Standing up, she winks as my jaw goes slack. "What, did you think she was really going to keep that secret?"

Shaking my head, I hold out my arm for her to loop hers through and we head toward the stairs. "I shoulda known. I guess Mom knows, too?"

"You bet she does." Gran throws her head back and laughs. "Etta swore all of us to secrecy. She thinks this one's a keeper."

Rolling my eyes, it's my turn to chuckle. "But Etta's not met her yet; how would she know?"

"You'll need to ask her that question." Pulling away from me, Gran starts down the stairs, then stops halfway and turns to look up at me, her eyes sparkling from the lights on the tree. "One last thing I'll say about love is that when you know, you know. Doesn't matter how long you have known someone." She pats her heart. "You'll feel it here and it's glorious; it'll slam into you like a freight train, and you'll be confused and overwhelmed, but you'll know. Oh my boy, if you are so lucky, you will know that it's her and it always will be."

She then reaches into her pocket and climbs back up the stairs to where I stand, pressing a small box into my hand. When I open the top, it reveals the engagement ring given to her by my Gramps.

"Here. This saves me from being buried with it or having to will it."

"Gran!"

"I'm kidding." She pats my hand. "It's for when you're ready," she whispers. "You'll know when."

Gran turns around and continues making her way downstairs to join the party. Clutching the banister, I stay put for a few minutes, watching my family and our close friends as they toast the holidays.

As I make my way downstairs to join everyone, the doorbell rings. I freeze with my foot in the air while Etta skips over to the door, throwing it open. She squeals and steps back, opening the door wide to let Maisey Montgomery in.

* * *

Maisey

I've waited all week for this moment. My hands tremble and I'm a little sick with excitement, but all going the way I intend, it's going to be worth it.

When Etta opens the door, some of my fear is assuaged. Her smile calms my nervous energy to a degree. Her arms wrap around me as she pulls me in for a hug.

"I'm so glad you finally got here." She shuffles backward, revealing the lively living room in all of its holiday glory. A room full of smiling faces, most I kind of know from the cafe but a lot of them new to me, all stare at me.

I mean, they STARE. To the point my armpits feel slick with perspiration. My eyes meet Etta's, and I'm already thinking of backing out of our plan. As if she can read my mind, she grabs my hand and pulls me over the threshold. "Get in here, you. We don't bite."

Before I can put my foot inside the door, I look over to the staircase and see him. Jack stands there looking at me, and he takes my breath away.

Blue eyes flash in my direction and a pink flush hits his cheeks. "Hi."

"Hey," I manage, giving him a little wave. I'm so aware there's a room packed with his people watching this whole thing right now. The Jack and Maisey show, here for your nightly viewing pleasure.

In one swift move, Jack bounds down the steps and grabs my hand, leading me outside. Before he can close the door behind him, Etta thrusts her body in the doorjamb and comes out to the front porch with us.

Jack looks at his sister, giving her an expression that I think is meant to say "back off." She's not getting it.

"No need for introductions," she says as she gives him a cheeky grin. "We've met."

Jack's head swivels on its axis and his eyes slam into mine. "You have?"

"We actually bumped into each other the same day we got back from Mistletoe Lodge." I cross my arms in front of my chest. "Literally ran into each other. Lucky for me, and for you, she was on her way to find me."

"Etta." Jack throws his hands in the air. "I asked you ages ago to stop playing Cupid for me."

"Shush. It was all for a good reason." She reaches out and squeezes my elbow. "I'll see you when you come inside. I've got a cup of eggnog with your name on it."

We watch the door close, turning to face each other once we're alone.

"So," Jack says.

"So." I stare at my feet. "I'm sorry I didn't talk to you this week. It's been really busy and, to tell you the truth, I needed time to think."

"I get that." Jack shifts his weight from one foot to the other. I feel his eyes watching my every move. "Looks like you had some extra help from my sister, though."

"She's awesome." I chuckle because she is. Between Etta, Dylan, and even my niece, Freya, I'd spent the better part of this week getting a confidence boost I desperately needed. "In fact, I'm surrounded by a support group of amazing women." My thoughts jump to Dub. "And men, too. I'm really lucky."

"Yeah?" Jack leans against the porch column. "Did they tell you to play hard to get and not call?"

"Ha." Wrapping my coat tighter around me, I step forward with the intention of smacking him playfully, but he catches my hand and we both freeze. Hand holding hand, he tugs me closer to him and wraps an arm around my waist. My body melts into his—but no, can't do this now. Not yet.

Stepping back, I clap my hands together in front of me. "What they told me was to stop playing games. They reminded me how awesome I am and that I shouldn't be afraid to go for what I want, no matter what."

Jack tilts his head to one side. "You know, I had a surprise conversation earlier that kind of was about the same thing."

"Hold on now, mister. Don't go stealing my thunder. This is my grand gesture, not yours."

Jack's eyes grow wide as his mouth drops open. "Grand gesture?"

"I know I talk a good game, but it's not only the man's job to show up in a relationship." I make my way down the front porch steps and stand on the sidewalk, leaving Jack on the porch looking down at me.

"Are you saying nobody puts baby in a corner?"

Oh, he is funny, isn't he?

"No, I'm saying nobody puts my fire daddy in a corner."

I'm funny, too.

Putting my hand in my jacket pocket, I pull out a small flashlight. Turning around, I face the street and blink the light twice. It's Dylan's signal it's time for her part of the drill.

"What are you—" Jack starts to say, but lights behind me blaze to life. He stops talking and can only stare.

During the week, I managed to get Dylan and Reid to help me decorate the ambulance with Christmas lights. Thanks to a tutorial on YouTube, we were able to form the words "I love you" in a glorious vision of twinkling red, blue, yellow, and green fairy lights. To help punctuate the moment, Reid turns on the ambulance lights while Dylan throws piles of fake snow out of the passenger-side window.

Turning around, I throw my arms out wide. "Ta da?"

Jack's stunned, not moving or speaking. At all. It's like he's gone into a comatose shock. I'm beginning to question my thought process that got me here when he smacks his hands together and starts laughing. He reaches for me, then stops. Holding up his finger giving me the universal "wait a minute" sign, he disappears on the other side of the front door only to reappear a moment later with a wrapped box clutched tightly in his hands.

"Here." He holds it out for me to take, which I do. "Merry Christmas, Maisey."

Never mind he's not said anything about the lights. I'm gonna stick to my non-assuming guns and open my present. Giddily, I tear the paper off and open the box to find one of the small snow globes from the Mistletoe Lodge inside.

"I picked this one out for you because of the small village

in there." He points to it and to the couple in the middle of the village. "That's us, and we're surrounded by a village because we live in one."

Laughing, I shake the globe and watch the snow swirl. "We really do."

With a sweet smile playing on his lips, Jack grins and watches as I tilt and swirl the globe some more. He points to its base. "But I really want you to look at the bottom. Turn it over."

Flipping it upside down, I freeze. There, on a small brass plaque, is an inscription.

I'm in love with you and it's that simple. Jack xo

My heart slams in my chest and my hand flutters to my throat. My eyes make their way to his, and I've never ever before felt so seen.

"Thank you." Clutching the snow globe, I hold it next to my heart. "This means the world to me. It's a great reminder of our trip to Mistletoe Lodge."

"I wanted you to always look at it and know it's the place where I officially fell in love with you." Jack pushes a strand of my hair out of my face as he tilts his head in the direction of the ambulance. "You did all of that, for me?"

"With help, obviously. Reid and Dylan were awesome, both of them wanted to help. Although I have a feeling Dylan talked Reid into it, but I'm not complaining."

Jack shakes his head, keeping his eyes trained on me. "I've been sweating this out, wondering how I could make some kind of gesture to you so you could see that I want to be with you, and you go and one-up me."

My mouth opens to retort, but the crackling of the radio in the ambulance interrupts us, followed by Reid's voice over the vehicles' external intercom.

"Ambo 85 is out, we have a fried turkey on fire a few blocks over." The engine comes to life with Dylan behind the wheel, but Reid's still going. He hangs out the window, his mouth still pressed to the microphone. "Jack, dude. You need to check your voicemail. Something weird is going on with your outgoing message."

They leave as efficiently as they arrived—reminding me there's an outgoing message I still need to contend with. However, not right now.

Jack steps forward, one hand snaking out as he hooks his finger through a belt loop and pulls me into him. His nostrils flare as I touch my hand to his chest, leaning my body into his and placing my forehead against his chin. The very touch of his skin on mine sends an eruption of volcanic lava-like heat rippling through my body.

We've already had one kiss, but this one is going to be different. I remind myself to stay steady, confident. We've worked pretty hard to get to this place and to this moment. I'm going to enjoy every minute.

I feel his hands slide to my hips, so I cup his face with my hands and tilt his head so we're looking into each other. Not at each other—that's what we did before. BM. Before Mistletoe. Now, we look *into* each other. I swear I can see his whole soul as clearly as I know he sees mine.

The gentle pressure from his hands tells me I'm safe, stable, and secure. Three words that resonate and scream Jack McCoy to me. What an absolute surprise this man has been and what a whirlwind. I'm in love with him and I want the world to know it.

As he comes closer to me, so close I feel his breath hitting my cheek, I part my lips and close my eyes. His lips find their way to my neck, skimming my skin and making my pulse quicken.

"You're a tease," I manage to growl, my voice husky.

"No," he says as he pulls away and drags his eyes to meet mine. "No more teasing."

His lips slant on top of mine, crashing into each other like two stars flying through space. His kiss is the sweetest taste I've had on my lips ever, and that includes a slice of chocolate chip pecan pie.

In this one moment with this one kiss, I see our future. I see the past. And I know that this guy is the one for me. My hand flutters to his cheek as he strokes mine, and our kisses begin to slow down in an effort for the two of us to catch our breath. As Jack pulls away, he reaches into his pocket and pulls out another box. This one is smaller, and it's a size and shape I'm familiar with.

"Now, wait," he says when he sees my mouth fall open. "Before you remind me we're not really engaged, I want to acknowledge that and tell you everyone in that house knows we aren't as well."

"Everyone?"

"Well..." He rocks his head from side to side, thinking. "Now that I think about it, only the ones that count. So everyone-ish. Everyone-adjacent."

"Okay." I giggle before kissing his cheek. "So, what about it?"

"This was my Gran's, like I told you. That part isn't a lie. When I get married, I'm using her ring, and tonight she gave it to me." He opens up the top of the small jewelry box to show me the diamond ring sitting on top of a small, pillow-like interior. "One day, and one day soon, I plan on asking you to marry me. But not yet. If it's okay with you, I'd like to go back inside and tell that asylum of mine we're putting our engagement on pause so we can date first."

I throw my head back and laugh. When my fit calms itself, our eyes find one another's. "I think that plan is the best one ever."

"Good." He slides the box into his pocket and, taking hold of both of my hands again, pulls me in hard to his body. His lips find mine and I'm back in my kissing dream-state if ever there was one before. It's amazing here and I don't want to leave.

"Hey." Jack slides his lips from mine, only to come back for one more quick peck. "It's cold out here and we really should get inside. Are you ready for this?"

I look at the front door and back to Jack, nodding my head. "I'm so ready to meet the Terror Twins."

"They're going to love you. You've already won Etta over, and she's half the battle."

He takes my hand and starts to open the door for me, but suddenly stops and closes it again. "I love you, Maisey Montgomery. I've not been good at communicating, I know, and I'm going to get better. If I've learned anything it's to make sure I let people know how I'm feeling so that assumptions don't hold things up."

Grinning, I stand on my tiptoes to kiss his cheek. "I love you, too, Jack. And you've had a heck of a year, so go easy on yourself. I'm here if you need me."

His lips find mine, one last time before he opens the door wide. As he does, his cell rings and he pulls it from his pocket. "This thing has been ringing all day!"

"About your voicemail..."

"Maisey, hand me your bouquet. You're going to drop it in the toilet if you try to take it in the bathroom with you."

"Take it from the woman who had her hand stuck in a toilet, she knows," Dylan laughs as she maneuvers out of the path of Ari's right hand.

"Oh, har har," Ari says as she snatches the flowers out of my hands and leans against the bathroom sink. "I'll wait right here for you. Since I don't need to catch the bouquet..."

"I don't care what you think you need," my niece Freya sings out cheerfully from her position on a chaise lounge. "We're all on the dance floor tonight, cause it's what brides-maids do. We dance, we try to catch the flowers, and we are here for general moral support and cheering. Right, Maisey?"

Looking at my group of friends, my tummy is hit with a flood of warmth. These women. Each of them mean some-thing special to me. I've seen Freya grow up and now move on with her childhood sweetheart, and Ari has rolled back into town and taken over our newspaper and the heart of her true love. Dylan stood beside me through thick and thin, and I'd do the same for her. I've got three of the best friends in the world.

"Hey." A muffled voice calls out as two knocks resonate on the bathroom door. "You guys in there? I'm getting lonely out here."

Freya sits up and leans over to unlock the door, allowing Etta inside. Seeing Etta is a reminder that while I do have three of the most amazing best friends ever in the history of best friends in here with me, I also have a new sister, too.

"Wow, it's crammed in here," Etta says with a giggle. "You know they're almost ready for your first dance as Mr and Mrs. McCoy."

Mrs. McCoy. I can get used to that.

Standing in front of the mirror, I take another quick look to make sure my hair's still in place and that my dress doesn't have a stray ketchup stain I've not seen yet. I swear, I can be in a sealed room wearing all white, no ketchup in sight, and I still get some on me.

"Okay." Turning around, I take the flowers back from Ari and point them at the bathroom door. "Let's get back out there."

"Didn't we come in here so you could go to the bathroom?" Freya asks.

"I said I have a meeting in the ladies room, which was a joke. Actually a reference to a song from ages ago, and you guys followed me so," I threw my hands in the air. "Here we are."

"Controlled chaos." Etta's head bobs up and down. "I like it."

There's another two raps on the door, only this time it's more forceful and carries more weight than Etta's.

"Who is it?" Dylan calls out.

"The husband."

Freya reaches out to open the door again, but I beat her to it as I cross the room with one giant leap. Flinging the door open, I stand in all of my bridal glory, holding out my dress as if I'm about to drop to the floor and curtsey.

Two big, blue eyes sparkle mischievously as Jack grins and holds out his hand. "It's time for our first dance. Can I convince you to come out here and join me for it?"

Behind me, four women swoon. Make it three, because his sister just gagged.

"I'd love to." Placing my hand in his, I allow Jack to guide me back out into the hallway before I turn around to the room. "I'll see you all on the dance floor in a few moments right?"

There's a chorus of "you bet!" and "yes, we'll be there" as the door closes behind me, leaving me alone with my new husband. I want to pinch myself. My head spins left and then right, double checking we're really alone, before throwing my arms around him and letting my fingers dance along the nape of his neck.

"Hi, Mr. McCoy."

"And hello, Mrs. Jack McCoy." His arms wrap around my waist and he pulls me closer to his body. I lay my head on his chest, sighing and letting my hands trail their way along his arms. I feel his strength reflected in the curves of his biceps as he kisses the top of my head.

"Fancy meeting you here." Pulling away, I thread my hand through one of his to keep our connection. Is it crazy I don't want to stop touching this man? Ever?

"Yes, very fancy." His eyes flick to the Mistletoe Lodge sign hanging on the wall. "I still can't believe you managed to get us a spot here for our wedding day. Even Gran is impressed. They're booked out years ahead of time."

"Lucky for us, Theo had some pull with Eileen." Not to self: send Theo a giant gift basket next week as a thank you.

"Yes, lucky for us."

I'm staring at Jack's lips when they curve into a smile. "Are you staring at my lips?"

Busted. I slowly nod my head. "I was thinking how marriage is sealed with a kiss."

"And now you want me to kiss those lips of yours, do you?" His voice is deep and rough like gravel, and my breath hitches. And I know at this very moment that I want to always feel that hitch inside me when I go to kiss this man.

His head leans in toward mine, and while I want to focus on his eyes I can't. It's all a blur and a rush of cool water blasts through my veins. One thing I've learned about Jack is that his mouth is skillful and he knows how to deliver some on pointe kisses, and I am here for all of them. Every one of them. For all time.

His mouth moves over mine and I fall into him, my hands snaking their way back around his neck to pull him in closer, because I want more. I want this moment, I want the dance we're about to have, I want a family with him––no matter what it looks like, as long as Jack's with me––I want it all.

As Jack's lips press with more firmness and need, I'm lost in them. But not so much I don't pull myself back to the present and the fact there's an announcement being made in the ballroom right now and we're supposed to be there taking our first dance.

Slowing the kiss down, I pull away slowly and deliberately, but with great sadness and a promise to come back later for more. Grinning, Jack presses his forehead to mine.

"Fine. Rain check it is." He straightens his jacket and takes my hand. "Ready?"

I glance down where my hand is cradle, snugly, inside his grasp. Where I want to be. Right here, with him.

Squeezing his hand, I stand on my tip toes to kiss his cheek one last time before we take the dance floor by storm.

"With you? I'm ready for anything."

****

Dylan

"Are you ready to dance now?" I say to Reid as soon as I get back to our table in the ballroom. I've been in the bathroom chatting with the other bridesmaids a little too long. We were supposed to join Maisey and Jack on the dance floor for our bridal party dance about sixty seconds ago.

"Are you kidding me?" Reid Shannon's chocolate brown eyes rise up to greet me. "I was born ready."

He stands up in one swift motion, grabs my hand and leads me onto the dance floor. No messing around with this one. I know him well enough to know that while he can't really dance, he will lead. So, I do that thing you do for your best friend. I let him.

The dance floor is full of couples, all swaying back and forth to the song. A few feet away, Jack spins Maisey and pulls her in close before leading her into a low dip, causing a ripple of laughter in the room.

"They're so good together," I murmur. "Makes me believe that true love is really out there, you know?"

"If it was, wouldn't we both be settled down by now?" Reid asks, firmly pressing his hands into my waist. "I mean, I know I'm a catch."

I jerk my head back ready to protest when I see the twinkle in his eye. Biting my lip, I shake my head. "You're actually a great catch Reid. You just haven't found the right partner yet."

"I need to find someone I can hang out with, who gets that I love being a fireman, who makes me laugh and doesn't want to take life too seriously, and they have to have patience."

"Okay, first off we'll talk about that list later. Secondly, why patience?"

Reid shrugs. "I'm not perfect, Dylan. I know I'll need some schooling when I finally find the one."

A flutter begins in my chest, working its way across my heart. Just hearing him say "find the one" makes my insides get gooey. "We're two lost souls swimming in a fish bowl..."

"Are you quoting Pink Floyd to me?" Reid's breath hits my neck, sending a shiver across my skin as the song playing comes to an end. What is that feeling for?

"...year after year," I manage to finish the lyric as I began to step away, but another song comes on and Reid reaches out and pulls me back into him.

"One more song with your best guy friend?" His lopsided grin is draped perfectly on those lips of his, who am I to say no.

"Fine." I wrap my arms around his neck and snuggle into him again. Since I moved to Lake Lorelei, Reid Shannon has been my go-to guy. When my dad introduced us, we hit it off instantly and lucky for me he's ended up being my partner for the days I ride on the ambulance for the fire department.

I'd be lying if I said I haven't had feelings for him. How can you spend as much time together as we have and not develop something––whether it's all lovey thoughts or irritation, you walk away with feeling.

Reid's hand rests on my lower back and his thumb makes a small circle against my spine, while somewhere deep inside my stomach a somersault begins. Something in this moment feels more intimate than others, but––come on.

Shaking it off, and telling the somersaults to slow it down, I close my eyes and try to relax. But there's a clean scent of fresh sheets and aftershave hitting my senses that is taking over.

I don't know if it's the ambiance around us or the general energy of the day, but something about Reid is different today. Not that he is different, but something about *him.* Maybe it's me. Something is different inside me today which wouldn't surprise me considering the fact we're surrounded by romance and love, celebrating the union of two very cool people who are also so in love you feel it when they walk into a room.

The tummy flips are back, and it's brought its friend confusion with it. I'm trying to ignore the fact that each time I focus my energy on where Reid's hands are, my insides quiver and I'm rocked with anticipation. Maybe it's anxiety?

The song comes to an end and, grateful for the reprieve, I step away but not before giving Reid a quick hug. I see his face twist into an odd shape as I dash away, back to our table. Am I suddenly being weird? I guess so but I had to find a way to clear my head and remind myself I'm not having a moment with my emotions.

Emotions having to do with Reid.

No. No. No.

"Hey." Etta stands beside me, tapping my arm. "Can I ask you a quick question?"

Relieved it's Jack's sister, and not Reid following me to ask me what's wrong, I nod my head enthusiastically. Maybe a bit too much because my neck hurts now. "Ask me anything."

"Okay, and please, if I'm stepping on your toes tell me." She leans in and points to where Reid stands chatting with some other members of the fire department. "Is he single?"

My eyes bounce to where she's pointing and then back to her. Again, they make their way back to where she points to Reid, and then they return to stare at Etta.

"Reid?" Managing to both keep my voice steady and also not to gulp, I keep my tone casual. I'm just the good friend of some guy and here's some girl who's asking about him. "Are you asking if he's single?"

"I am. Is it weird?" she asks.

Well, I certainly can't tell her the weird part is that I've been confronted, only moments ago, with my own feelings about the man in question. Etta's also really nice, she's Jack's twin and she's talking about moving here——and, with those thoughts running through my head, it all just got more complicated than I need it to be.

"It's not weird." *Just deflating*. "Reid's single."

"So he's not dating anyone?"

"Nope." Pulling out my chair, I plop down onto it. "He dates, but nothing serious."

I'm feeling calmer as I sip on my water and stab my fork into the wedding cake that made its way to my seat at some point while I was dancing. Taking a bite, I chew thoughtfully, watching Etta as she stands up a little taller and smooths her bridesmaid's dress.

"Well, I'm going to ask him to dance. Wish me luck?"

"Luck!" I call out, waving my fork in the air as she walks away. Thrusting my fork back into the cake to dig out another sugar hit, I watch as she makes her way over to the small group, pulls Reid aside and speaks with him. In a few moments, he takes her hand and leads her onto the dance floor.

Watching them weave their way onto the ballroom floor, a pit forms in my middle. Taking another forkful, I slowly raise it to my mouth and wouldn't you know it; I'm grateful I can eat my emotions at this very moment. I'm watching Etta's arms snarl their way around Reid's neck, as his hands take her by the waist and he holds her tenderly.

I'm mid swallow when it hits me like a boulder falling off a cliff. This feeling I'm having, the confusion.

Somewhere along the way, in between being good friends

and being *great* friends, it appears I managed to fall in love with my best friend.

Now what do I do?

Don't miss How to Fall in Love with your Best Friend, Dylan and Reid's story!

Thank you!

Saying thank you to all of the people who helped me get this book out is seriously the least I can do...each and everyone of the folks listed below are people in my life who helped me get this baby out this year!

Every author needs a support staff. Mine consists of some amazing friends (looking at you, Writer Frenz!) who will help me brainstorm when I hit a wall or life me up when I'm doubting if I can type another word. This tribe gives me LIFE and I'm beyond grateful for you!

My husband. You patient man, you. Thank you for feeding me, listening when I repeat over and over "I'm reviewing. I'm revising. I'm editing...wash. Rinse. Repeat." You're an angel and I don't say thank you enough, so instead I'll type it. Love you.

My editor Sara Dawn Johnson is spectacular and I love that she's in my world. Same for you, Sabrina Rivera. It's hard to find a PA in general, but finding one halfway around the world who gets me and can make magic like you do? BRILLIANT!

The biggest thank you of all goes to my ARC team and my readers. Your encouragement, notes, emails, tags in social media posts, DMs, etc, etc...YOU keep me going. I show up and type to tell the story because I want us (my little village) to all be in on the joke together. To know the people of Lake Lorelei, and to go on this journey together. It's more fun when you do it with a group, you know?

Thank you - and happy reading!
Anne x

Also by Anne Kemp

Love in Lake Lorelei Series

Sweet RomComs sizzling with chemistry and bringing you all the feels. Get to know this small town, its locals and, most importantly, the Lake Lorelei Fire Department!

Sweet Summer Nights (Book 1)

Freya and Wyatt's story

The Sweet Spot (Book 2)

Ari and Carter's story

When Sparks Fly (Book 3)

Maisey and Jack's story

How to Fall in Love with Your Best Friend (Book 4)

Dylan and Reid's story

coming March 2023!

Stay up-to-date on new releases, get special bonus content, and special promotions when you sign up for

Anne's newsletter: http://eepurl.com/cCEKUT

Anne Kemp is an author of romantic comedies, sweet contemporary romance, and chick lit.
She loves reading (and does it ridiculously fast, too!), gluten-free baking
(because everyone needs a hobby that makes them crazy), and finding time to binge-watch her favorite shows. She grew up in Maryland but made Los Angeles her home until she encountered her own real-life meet-cute at a friend's wedding where she ended up married to one of the groomsmen.
For real.

Anne now lives on the Kapiti Coast in New Zealand, and even though she was married at Mt. Doom, no...she doesn't have a Hobbit. However, she and her husband do have a terrier named George Clooney and a rescue pup named Charlie. When she's not writing, she's usually with them taking a long walk on the river by their home.

You can find Anne on her website www.annekemp.com or find her on social media.
She's on TikTok andInstagram as @annekempauthor
and on Facebook and Twitter @missannekemp.

www.ingramcontent.com/pod-product-compliance
Lightning Source LLC
Chambersburg PA
CBHW031631130726
47900CB00019B/2460